PRAISE FOR IRIS MORLAND

HE LOVES ME, HE LOVES ME NOT

A hilarious, sexy and heartwarming romantic comedy...you do not want to miss this fun, feel-good romance.

— MARY DUBÉ, CONTEMPORARILY EVER AFTER

...refreshing, funny, emotionally charged, and very entertaining to read.

— CAROL, TIL THE LAST PAGE

There is humor, there is heart and there is heat in this story! I absolutely loved it! . . . Mari and Liam delivered. Yowza, their chemistry was palpable.

— BIBLIOPHILE CHLOE

PETAL PLUCKER

Funny, charming, and utterly captivating! I devoured this sparkling read.

— ANNIKA MARTIN, NEW YORK TIMES
BESTSELLING AUTHOR

Petal Plucker was funny, entertaining, fresh and fan-yourself-worthy . . . Their enemies-to-lovers romance is both charming, tender and steamy, and you'll love both of these characters (and their families!) and their sigh-worthy happily ever after.

— MARY DUBÉ, CONTEMPORARILY EVER AFTER

Morland has created a masterpiece of a romance . . . one of my favorite [books] of the year.

— CRISTIINA READS

Humorous, raunchy, and refreshing, Petal Plucker has rightfully earned its way, in my opinion, as one of the best romantic comedy [books] this year.

— CAROL, TIL THE LAST PAGE

My One and Only

This book was gripping, well written & the chemistry between the characters sizzled throughout this wonderful read.

— AMAZON REVIEW

All I Want Is You

Another heartfelt, steamy, terrific story. This is an author who really knows how to create a story that catches a reader's attention and characters that capture her heart.

— BOOKADDICT

TAKING A CHANCE ON LOVE

Thea and Anthony are in for a surprise when it comes to the language of the heart . . . I am in awe.

— HOPELESS ROMANTIC BLOG

THEN CAME YOU

This story really pulled all my heartstrings. This was truly a beautiful story and makes you believe there really is true love out there.

— MEME CHANELL BOOK CORNER

ALSO BY IRIS MORLAND

HERON'S LANDING

Say You're Mine

All I Ask of You

Make Me Yours

Hold Me Close

THE FLOWER SHOP SISTERS

Oopsie Daisy

He Loves Me, He Loves Me Not

Petal Plucker

War of the Roses

LOVE EVERLASTING

including

THE YOUNGERS

Then Came You

Taking a Chance on Love

All I Want Is You

My One and Only

THE THORNTONS

The Nearness of You

The Very Thought of You

If I Can't Have You

Dream a Little Dream of Me

Someone to Watch Over Me

Till There Was You

I'll Be Home for Christmas

MAKE ME YOURS

HERON'S LANDING

IRIS MORLAND

BLUE VIOLET PRESS LLC

CONTENTS

For my sister.

MAKE ME YOURS

This book is a work of fiction. The names, characters, places and incidents are products of the writer's imagination or have been used fictitiously and are not to be constructed as real. Any resemblance to persons, living or dead, actual events, locales or organizations is entirely coincidental.

Make Me Yours (Heron's Landing Book 3)
Published by Blue Violet Press LLC
Seattle, Washington

Copyright © 2016, 2020 by Iris Morland
Cover design by Qamber Designs

All rights reserved. No part of this book may be reproduced in any form or by any electronic or mechanical means, including information storage and retrieval systems, without written permission from the author, except for the use of brief quotations in a book review.

Published 2020.

First edition published 2016 under the title Desire Me Dearly (Heron's Landing Book 3). Second edition 2020.

Dear Readers,

Before you begin Gavin and Kat's story, please know that *Make Me Yours* was previously published under the title *Desire Me Dearly*. This second edition has been edited and expanded to include 20% more content than the original.

The main storyline remains the same as the first edition, but I always felt Gavin and Kat's story needed more.

All my best,
Iris

On the first day of classes, Kat Williamson cursed the humidity rampant in August and hoped her hair hadn't turned into a ball of frizz before nine AM. Although the school where she taught computer classes to elementary students had AC, it struggled to keep up when the temperatures reached above one hundred, which was pretty common this time of year in Missouri.

Kat hustled to the staff room. The copy machine always had a line this close to the bell. Normally Kat arrived earlier, but she'd woken up late and had had to hustle it to get to school on time. Two other teachers were ahead of Kat, and of course one of them ended up getting the copier jammed.

Kat sighed inwardly. *Today's going to be a mess, isn't it?* Luckily, she didn't have to teach until later that morning, but she still needed to finish her lesson plans. Normally she was way more organized, but she'd been distracted last night with messing with closing her grandmother's cell phone account. Apparently telling someone the account holder was deceased wasn't enough of a reason to close said account, Kat had found out to her immense frustration.

"Coffee?"

Kat turned to see her fellow teacher and friend, Silas Fraser, standing at her elbow. He was about her height, with light brown hair and a gap-toothed grin, and one of the few teachers around her age. They'd bonded over their Millennial status and griped about how no one in this school knew how to use a computer. Most of the teachers here were almost twice Kat's age—not a bad thing, necessarily, but sometimes there was a bit of a culture gap.

"Yes, thank you," she replied, taking the steaming mug. Normally she brought her own coffee, but apparently today was not going to go how it normally did. She sipped it and made a face. "God, that's awful."

Silas laughed. "It's Folgers from 1994. I think." He gazed at his own mug. "I think they stopped buying fresh coffee then. You know the school won't even buy us creamer because it's a 'luxury.'"

Kat rolled her eyes. Right then, the teacher who'd jammed the copier managed to pull the offending paper and get the copier going again. The second the teacher finished, Kat practically wrapped herself around the copier: *mine, don't touch!*

Silas laughed at her. "I thought you knew better than to make copies right now."

"Yeah, I know. It's my own fault." Kat tapped her foot. "Why is this thing so slow?"

"It's older than me, that's why," said Silas.

"That seems to be a theme in this school." After Kat's copies printed, she grabbed the papers and her cooling cup of coffee.

"Wait, before you go," said Silas shyly. He looked around, like he didn't want anyone to overhear. If so, he'd picked the worst spot imaginable, as everyone was currently running around in circles in the break room, wondering where their things were, why the coffee tasted terrible, and complaining that it was so hot in here no matter how much they complained about the crappy air conditioners

Kat barely suppressed her impatience, but Silas was a friend. "Shoot."

"Do you want to get a drink sometime?" A blush crawled up Silas's face as he said the words, and he cleared his throat before adding, "You know, like a date."

She blinked. She'd been expecting him to ask her to cover bus duty this week or something. Silas had been most decidedly in the friend category in her mind—not because he wasn't dateable, but because he hadn't shown the least interest in her up until now. She sipped her coffee again, mostly because she was figuring out what to say.

"I don't think that would be a good idea," she finally said. She saw him blushing harder and instantly felt guilty. "I mean, I would, but with my grandmother and everything…" She trailed off, hoping he'd get the hint.

Luckily, he did. "No, I get it. But think about it, okay? You don't have to say yes or no right now." He handed her the last of her copies. "See you later, Kat."

Despite her best efforts, Kat couldn't help but think about another man as she walked to her class. A man she wished would ask her out.. Gavin Danvers, who'd avoided her since he'd been so awkward at the farm-to-table festival earlier in the spring.

Not only had Gavin fallen on top of her to keep a ball from

hitting her, but he'd looked at her lips for an intensely long moment—like he'd wanted to kiss her. Until he'd sprung up like he'd been scalded and had subsequently avoided her. Considering Heron's Landing was ridiculously tiny, avoiding a particular person took a lot of effort. And Kat had definitely noticed Gavin's effort in this regard.

Gavin was the black sheep of the Danvers' family. While his brother Adam Danvers ran the family vineyard, Gavin had moved away with his wife and daughter years ago. But now Gavin was back, newly divorced, his young daughter with him.

Kat wondered if Gavin had ever asked a woman out for drinks, or if he just smoldered in their general direction and they came running. Then again, he'd been married at a young age. He might not have a lot of dating experience.

By the time it was time for Kat to teach an hour later, she'd gotten her brain in order, as well as her lesson plans. Kat had been able to stop thinking about Gavin Danvers—until Kat saw his young daughter Emma was one of the kids in her class. *Of course she is*, Kat thought to herself.

Considering that the elementary school in Heron's Landing had all of one class per grade, it was pretty much guaranteed that Kat would be teaching Emma Danvers at some point today or tomorrow.

Today, Emma had her hair in lopsided braids, wearing purple leggings under an orange dress. At eight, the girl picked out her own clothes, but their lack of coordination, as well as the hair that was messy and probably completely tangled, bespoke a father who was distracted, to say the least. Kat rather wished she could come to their place and braid the girl's hair herself.

Emma didn't look much like her father, but sometimes her mannerisms would mirror his. She tended to narrow her eyes like Gavin would when annoyed. Both father and daughter also preferred to observe first and speak later. Kat had a feeling that Emma's was more due to shyness, whereas her father's was more because he found small talk annoying.

Emma said no more than five words the entire class, never raising her hand when Kat asked a question. Kat never cold-called on students—humiliation never worked as a learning tool—but she tried to get as many of her students involved as possible. It was too easy for some to disappear in the crowd, though. Kat knew she needed to find a way to get the shyer students to interact along with the more extroverted ones.

While the kids did work on their own, Kat stopped by each student to encourage them or correct their finger place-ment on the keyboard. When Kat got to Emma, she watched as the girl typed the sentence on the screen perfectly and as quickly as any adult.

"Where did you learn to type like that?" said Kat, impressed.

Emma jumped, her fingers smashing into the keyboard. Her eyes were wide as she looked up at Kat.

Kat touched Emma's shoulder. "Sorry, sorry! I didn't mean to sneak up on you like that."

Where most kids would shrug or laugh, Emma just shook her head and seemed to turn further into herself. She tipped her chin down and said in a low voice, "My mom."

Kat squatted down next to Emma. "Your mom?"

"She showed me how to type."

"Oh, well, she did a great job. I couldn't type that fast when I was your age."

"She used to be a secretary."

Kat was tempted to keep asking questions about Gavin's ex-wife and Emma's mother, but she bit her tongue. It was none of her business, even though she was dying to know why they'd divorced and why Gavin had gotten custody of Emma. Didn't mothers usually get custody?

Curiosity killed the cat, Kat reminded herself.

Kat watched Emma for the rest of the class. She seemed especially jumpy even toward the end of class. When one of her classmates accidentally kicked over a thankfully empty metal trashcan, the sound resounding through the room, Emma practically ran out of the room.

Did Gavin know about this behavior? Kat wondered as the day progressed onward, unsure if it was her place to say anything when it wasn't as if Emma had done anything wrong.

By the time Kat arrived home close to five o'clock, she was exhausted. She was tempted to take a nap, but she knew if she gave in to the indulgence, she'd never sleep later that night.

The house still seemed eerily empty without her grandmother, Lillian Jacobs, and as Kat made dinner, she had to stop herself from making enough food for two. But it was just her now, wasn't it? Suddenly too tired to finish making the soup she'd started, she pulled out a frozen dinner and popped it into the microwave. Staring at the meal as it circled around, she wondered if this was a metaphor for her life: circling and circling but never getting anywhere.

Lillian had passed only a month ago at the age of eighty-five. She'd been as spirited upon her deathbed as she had been in life, telling Kat that she didn't want her to cry after her death because she was going to a better place, and besides, she was old. Old people died. She'd patted Kat's hand, and after that, she'd returned to that strange place in her mind that had been overtaken by dementia, not recognizing her granddaughter at the very end.

Kat had inherited her grandmother's house and some money from her life insurance policy, and now that it was almost fall, she wasn't sure if she wanted to sell the house or not. She'd considered it. She had no use for a house older than she was, filled with cat figurines and unfinished knitting projects and a pantry brimming with canned goods that were as old as the house. But every time she returned to the house —no, *her* house, Kat supposed—she didn't have the heart to go through with a sale.

A few days ago, she'd stood in Lillian's pink kitchen with its retro appliances, flipping through old cookbooks. The pages had been sticky with use, and Kat had found one of the cookie recipes that Lillian had made for her as a child: potato chip cookies. She'd gotten the ingredients to make them herself but hadn't gotten around to it yet.

Kat missed Lillian fiercely, but she was also glad that she hadn't suffered for years. Her dementia had been clouding her mind for many years, and more and more, she'd had difficulty recognizing loved ones. Having her grandmother gaze at her like she was some stranger had broken Kat's heart.

A computer programmer by trade, Kat had attended UCLA before working at a tech start-up in the Valley. But when she'd gotten a call from a concerned friend who'd told her that Lillian could no longer live on her own and would have to be put in a home, Kat had packed up her things and moved to Missouri. She'd lived in Heron's Landing briefly as a child, before her mom had passed away from breast cancer when Kat had been fifteen. But it was a distant memory; she was a California girl at heart and missed Los Angeles rather desperately.

But right now, Kat was just getting melancholy over a TV dinner. Would everything make her cry? She suddenly couldn't eat in the living room: it hurt too much.

Instead, Kat went to her bedroom to eat and to work on her most recent video game she'd been creating. She had started making video games earlier that year, mostly to distract herself from her grandmother's declining health. Sitting down at her computer, she ate her TV dinner of pasta and broccoli, fiddling with code and making the finishing touches on the game she'd been working on ever since Lillian had passed away.

She pushed her glasses up her nose as she peered at the screen. It wasn't a complicated game by any means: the entire point was to keep a flying squirrel from hitting any obstacles and falling from the sky. It was a 2D game, reminiscent of the original Mario games. Kat had been working on more levels, enjoying the creative aspect of the game. She'd created levels where it looked like a jungle, another level where it looked like outer space. At the moment, she was testing the game for bugs and would hopefully post the game as a beta version on different forums for people to play around with later tonight.

If she were honest, Kat didn't expect anyone really to play her game. At most, she thought she might get a few hits here and there, a few comments on possible bugs. She went to bed feeling happy with her finished game while trying to keep her mind from thinking about Gavin Danvers and his daughter being in her class.

When Kat checked her phone the following morning to

see if anyone had tried out her game, she was delighted to see tons of comments on one of her forum posts. The delight soon turned to dismay as she began to read them, though.

You copied this game this isn't even original

y would u think this is a good idea this is the stupidest fucking thing

this is why women should stay in the kitchen lol stop making shit games and go make me a sandwich

PLAGARIST!!!

The comments, often full of misspellings, continued, each just as and derogatory as the last. Kat's stomach sank to her toes. She'd expected some trolls—it was the Internet, after all—but this bombardment? Over a silly game? She suddenly felt extremely naïve and stupid for posting the game in the first place.

Plus, it was a game about a *flying squirrel!* How would that be controversial? Her mind boggled. And she most certainly hadn't copied anyone, although she acknowledged that the idea surrounding it was hardly innovative.

Kat was about to delete the game entirely, but something stopped her. Was she really going to let some online bullies discourage her? She hadn't done anything wrong. She hadn't plagiarized anyone, that was for certain. Besides, as far as she knew, you couldn't literally plagiarize a video game—could you?

She snorted, reported all of the comments as abuse, and got ready for work.

CHAPTER TWO

Gavin Danvers shaded his eyes against the bright September sun. The heat of summer still lingered, and the humidity had crept up since this morning, making the air viscous against his skin. It was better than working inside, though, and after his boss back in Boston had given him an ultimatum—either return or find a new job—he'd decided he'd rather find a new job. He'd worked at a construction company, mostly doing administrative work, but it hadn't been particularly interesting nor fulfilling. Leaving that job for good hadn't been much of a sacrifice in the long run.

He wiped his forehead and continued hammering at the fence post. After quitting his job, he'd gone straight to Adam to ask for a job at the family vineyard, River's Bend. Adam had told him he didn't have any office jobs, but he could help around the vineyard itself if he wanted. Gavin had agreed without protest.

The labor allowed him to stop thinking for once. To stop thinking about Emma, about Teagan, about Emma's pretty teacher who had been so soft underneath him that bright afternoon back in the spring…

He wondered sometimes if he should've kissed her, just to have a smidgeon of pleasure amidst everything that had happened in the last year. Kat represented everything good and beautiful and peaceful, and he hungered for her like he'd never experienced in his entire life.

He hammered the nail into the post harder than necessary. He did not get to fantasize about Kat Williamson. He didn't get to imagine how soft her skin was, or how plump her lips were. He didn't get to imagine how she'd look in his bed, warm and supple and beautiful.

He had to remind himself that his divorce had only been finalized earlier this summer, and the last thing he should do was get into another relationship. Although his mind reasoned that his marriage had been over for ages anyway, so really, he'd been single for at least three years.

He and Teagan had met in high school and had dated starting their junior year. Bright and sunny with yellow-blonde hair, Teagan had been his dream girl. She'd been a cheerleader, and he'd been shocked when she agreed to go out with him. Adam had always been the popular brother, not Gavin. Gavin was too awkward, too reticent, preferring to keep his nose in a book rather than talk to girls. But Teagan had seen something in him he hadn't even realized was there, and he'd fallen in love with her by the time they were seniors.

They'd married soon after graduating from college, when they were both twenty-two. There'd been signs that Teagan was struggling: her moods would shift rapidly, high to low without any apparent trigger. Some days she'd spend all day in bed, barely eating or doing much of anything except staring at the wall, practically catatonic with despair. Then other days she'd be her bright, sunny self, and Gavin would hope that she'd remain that way. Everyone had bad days, he'd reasoned. Perhaps she had more bad days than others.

After Emma had been born, though, everything changed. Gavin had watched as his world—his family—had fallen apart, and there'd been nothing he could do to stop it. He'd tried— God knows he'd tried. But the life he thought he'd have with Teagan had slipped through his fingers like sand through a sieve.

That was all in the past, though. He moved down the line of the fence he was repairing, carrying tools and nails as he went. A hawk circled in the sky overhead, and the heat of the sun beat down on his neck and shoulders. It was the first time in a while that he'd felt truly alive.

Nothing like some physical labor to get a man's blood stirring again.

The day waned on, and as Gavin was about to finish the north side of the fence, he saw Adam walking toward him. He and Adam looked much alike, with their similar height and dark hair. Anyone could tell they were brothers at a swift glance. Adam, though, seemed to radiate happiness lately, and that difference between him and Gavin was stark at times. Adam and his fiancée Joy were getting married around Christmas, and although he had seemed rather overwhelmed with Joy's attention to various wedding details, he'd been undeniably happy. The love between them was obvious to anyone with eyes.

Gavin rather envied his brother at the moment. Hell, he'd envied—and not understood—Adam since they'd been kids.

"There you are," Adam said as he approached. His face was

creased in concern, which put Gavin on high alert. "Why the hell do you never answer your phone?"

"I didn't bring it out here with me."

Adam sighed. "Well, just as well. I got a call from the school. There's been an incident with Emma."

Gavin's blood ran so cold he was certain icicles were dripping from his fingers. God, how many times had he heard those words in regards to Emma's mother? *There's been an incident. Something's happened. You need to come right away.*

"Jesus Christ, why are you just standing there? I have to go." Gavin dropped everything into the grass and jogged back to the main building of the vineyard, not caring if Adam followed or not. His mind raced with every possibility: Had Emma been injured? Had she hurt herself? Oh God, what if she'd done something like what Teagan had done…?

"Hey, Gavin." Adam curled a hand around his arm to stop him before he entered the building. "You didn't let me finish. She's okay, but the nurse said she probably should go home."

Gavin panted. Adam's words helped the panic subside, but only slightly. He pulled his arm from his brother's grip. It was stupid, but he wanted to rail at Adam, demand to know why he hadn't cared when Gavin and his family had been splintering apart, with Teagan descending further into her bipolar disorder. But he kept his mouth shut, because it didn't matter.

Emma was what mattered.

"I have to go," he said gruffly, stalking off. He grabbed his things from inside and then drove to the school without even seeing where he was going, his heartbeat racing a mile a minute. He tried to get himself to climb off of the ledge, but it was almost impossible.

After Emma had discovered Teagan lying on the cold bathroom floor, having overdosed from too many painkillers, the young girl had struggled. Gavin had seen it, and his heart broke at how his daughter had retreated into herself. That had been the last straw. He'd told Teagan she needed to get help, and she'd finally broken down and realized the same, but not before insisting they get a divorce.

"You deserve to be free, find a new life for yourself," she'd said, her face drawn and pained. "I haven't been the wife or mother you both needed."

He parked his truck and practically ran inside the school. The elementary wing was on the south side, and he barreled down the mostly deserted hallways. Adam had said something about the nurse, so he would go there first.

When he entered the nurse's station, he didn't see Emma at first. He saw a teenage boy icing his elbow and another young girl crying as a woman placed a bandage on her knee. Then he saw her, and his knees almost gave out underneath him.

"Emma," he breathed. He kneeled in front of her, taking her hands, which were like ice. "Emma, what happened?"

The girl had wedged herself into a corner, like if she curled in on herself enough, she could disappear. Her big blue eyes stared at Gavin, and her gaze reminded him so much of Teagan his heart clenched. He rubbed her fingers. "Emma, sweetheart, talk to me."

The nurse came over. "You're Mr. Danvers, yes?"

He stood up. "Yes, I am. Do you know what happened? Is she all right?"

The nurse, a woman in her forties with graying hair, pursed her lips at his question. "She was found by a teacher in one of the supply closets. She wasn't present when the children were counted after lunch."

"And you didn't think to inform me that my daughter had disappeared?"

"By the time we realized she was gone, she'd been discovered." The woman glanced at Emma behind him. "She refused to tell me or anyone else what had happened, or why she decided to go hiding." Her voice lowered, but not low enough that everyone else in the small room couldn't hear her. "Have you thought about some kind of…assistance with her? She's, well, she's a bit odd, no?"

By this point, Gavin was seeing red. He knew he couldn't strangle a nurse—no matter how much he wanted to—so instead, he said in a low voice, "My daughter is not *odd*, and you can keep your opinions to yourself, ma'am." He turned and took Emma's hand. "Let's go home, sweetheart."

The nurse didn't say anything as they left the room, except to harrumph under her breath, like they'd tracked mud through her living room.

Emma followed, not letting go of his hand. She'd once been a happy, vibrant child, but she'd become so shy and reticent as of late that Gavin was at a loss as to what to do. Oh, he'd taken her to all the requisite therapists after Teagan's overdose, but they'd made the situation worse. Emma would refuse to speak for days after each session, sometimes hiding underneath the stairwell or her bed, Gavin discovering her and having to coax her out like a terrified animal. It was almost like she was a shy toddler instead of a second grader, hiding behind Gavin more often than not.

As he hurried Emma out, he saw a flash of bright green,

and then Kat Williamson was walking toward them, concern etched in her expression.

"Mr. Danvers, good, I'm so glad to see you." She softened her voice as she addressed Emma. "How are you feeling?"

Emma pressed her face into Gavin's arm. He touched her shoulder. "Answer the question, please."

She blinked those large blue eyes, rather like a snowy owl. "I'm okay," she whispered.

Kat didn't seem remotely convinced. Her gaze returned to Gavin, and he drank her in. He couldn't help it: from her dark, curly hair in its Afro to her bright magenta lips to her green dress with boots, she was pretty as a picture. Her skin practically glowed, too. She was way too pretty for Gavin's peace of mind.

"Can I talk to you privately for a second?" she asked.

He mostly just wanted to get home with his daughter, but he told Emma to go sit on a nearby bench, handing her his phone to play games on.

"Did they tell you I was the one who found her?" When his eyes widened, she made a noise in the back of her throat. "Figures. But I thought you'd like to know what happened, or at least what I could glean before they took her away to the nurse's office."

She looked around and drew him to a more private corner, although he could still keep an eye on Emma as they talked.

He closed his eyes for a moment, feeling weary to his bones. When would things turn around? When could he catch a breath for once?

"Hey, you okay?" Kat touched his arm.

Her touch sent an electric charge through his body, and he opened his eyes to see her looking at him with an expression of concern. His gut twisted. It was an expression he'd seen too much of in the last year.

"Tell me what happened," he said, even though there was a small, cowardly part of him that almost didn't want to know the answer.

After finishing her lunch in the teacher's lounge, Kat had headed to the restroom before returning to her classroom for the rest of the afternoon. As she passed a supply closet, she noticed that the door was cracked open, but there was no janitor in sight. She knew the cleaning staff never left the door unlocked or open in case kids wandered inside and played with things they shouldn't, and as she was about to shut the door, she saw movement in the corner.

Her heart stuttered. A rat? Maybe a raccoon that had gotten in last night? Or had a kid gotten inside? She walked in, flicking on the light overhead, and scanned the room. She saw a flash of pink in the corner. Kat was about to reprimand whoever had decided playing in the supply closet had been a good idea when she saw that the child in question was huddled on the floor, her head in between her knees, completely still and quiet, even as Kat approached.

"Emma," she breathed, kneeling in front of her. She touched her shoulder gently so as not to startle the girl, who looked up but didn't say anything. "Emma, what are you doing in here?"

Emma stared at her, like she didn't understand the words. The girl's face was pale and tear-streaked.

"Come on, let's get out of here," Kat coaxed. She tried to draw Emma up, but the girl pulled away and curled in on herself.

Kat was at a loss. Should she carry Emma from the room? But surely that would only make things worse. The girl looked like she'd seen a ghost or something.

"Emma, we need to get out of here. This isn't a nice place to talk."

Emma shook her head and mumbled something under her breath. Kat leaned toward her, trying to make out the girl's words.

"Can't leave," Emma mumbled over and over to herself. "It's not safe."

Now Kat was on high alert. She pulled out her phone and texted Silas to let him know what was going on before sitting down in front of Emma, taking her hands from her face. "What's not safe? Can you tell me?"

Emma just shook her head.

"Maybe we can figure out how to stay safe together, if you'll tell me."

Emma looked embarrassed suddenly, biting her lower lip as she gazed up at Kat. Kat waited, hoping she'd tell her what was wrong so Kat could figure out how to help. But instead, Emma just hugged her knees tighter and kept shaking her head over and over again. When she started crying and telling Kat she wanted her dad, Kat knew she couldn't do anything else for her. She was able to get her to stand so she could take her to the nurse's office.

Now, standing in front of Gavin, Kat struggled to find the words to explain what she'd seen. She didn't really know, if she was honest. She'd never seen a child so petrified, like she'd scream at her own shadow. She glanced at Emma sitting on the bench, seemingly normal and unafraid now.

"When I found her in the closet, it was like she was in shock," Kat explained. "She kept saying something about it not being safe. I don't know what happened, or what she saw."

Gavin's face was drawn, and he looked absolutely exhausted. She knew his divorce had been finalized in the last few months; she couldn't imagine having to care for a daughter who seemed so scared all the time.

She restrained herself from reaching out and taking his hand, reassuring him. He seemed so lonely standing there in front of her, like the weight of the world was on his shoulders.

"Did she say anything else to you?" His voice was almost toneless.

"Not really. When she started crying, I took her straight to the nurse. I didn't know what else to do." She hesitated a moment before asking, "Has this happened before?"

He sighed, pushing a hand through his dark hair, which had grown long and almost unruly lately. He still wore a beard, but it only emphasized his high cheekbones and chiseled jaw. Kat had never had an opinion about guys having facial hair or not, but she had to admit, it worked on Gavin Danvers.

"Emma hasn't been the same since we left Boston. Not since her mother..." He shook his head. "She's had episodes like this, where she hides and refuses to come out. But when I try to get her to tell me what happened, she says nothing happened."

Kat frowned. "It just happens out of the blue?"

He shrugged. "As far as I can tell. I think it may be linked to what happened with her mother." He grimaced, his expression darkening. "Actually, I know it is. There's no other reason for it."

Kat almost asked what had happened with his ex-wife, but she stopped herself. It was none of her business. She'd heard whispers that Teagan Danvers had had issues, but nothing beyond that. Besides, Kat was hardly family or even a close friend. She was Emma's teacher, and that was it. She didn't have a right to pry, no matter how much she wanted to understand not only the situation, but the man in front of her.

Gavin leaned against the wall. "I can't do this again," he murmured, almost to himself.

God, her heart broke for this man. She knew all too well what it felt like to watch loved ones hurt and not be able to do anything about it. She'd been the one to take care of her mom in her final days. She imagined Gavin had cared for Teagan in a similar way, giving up on his own hopes and dreams to try to keep another person living just another day. One more day, one more hour, one more minute, your life passed you by because another person needed you more.

Now, though, Kat was at a loss. She didn't know how she could help Gavin, or if she could help him.

You can't save everyone, her grandmother's words echoed in her mind. *Sometimes you have to just save yourself.*

He stood up from the wall and said, "Thank you for all your help. I think I need to get Emma home now."

She wished she could *do* something, but instead she replied, "If you need anything, let me know. Please."

Gavin gazed at her, his dark eyes drinking her in. He reached toward her and touched her hand, but then seemed to think better of it. "Thank you, Kat. For everything."

The moment seemed to enclose them in an intimate bubble, where it was only them gazing at each other, hoping for something different to happen. Hoping and wishing that life wasn't simply a series of hard knocks to be gotten over, but instead had beautiful, bright spots blooming in between that could provide succor during the difficult times.

His gaze moved to her lips, and her heart sped up. They were at school and she was his daughter's teacher and the last thing she should want was for him to kiss her right here and now, but she wanted him to. She wished he would.

But instead, he flicked is gaze away and the moment splintered. Reality intruded, hard and relentless.

"I should go," he said.

She watched as he and Emma walked out of the school, her bright, blonde hair a stark contrast to his darker features.

"Hey, you all right?"

Kat turned to see Silas next to her. She hadn't even heard him come up to her. She couldn't help but look back at Gavin's retreating figure before sighing.

"I guess. I wish I could help somehow."

Silas didn't say anything for a moment. He stuffed his hands in his trouser pockets, looking at his feet. "Is it your responsibility to help?" he asked quietly.

Kat didn't know how to take that question. "No, not really. But I want to anyway."

He frowned a little. "I hope you know what you're doing, is all."

"What do you mean?"

"Just that sometimes people aren't what they seem."

She sighed. "And now you're talking in riddles."

"Have you noticed the way he looks at you?" When she didn't reply, he added, "He looks at you like he wishes he could make you his own."

She couldn't help it—she laughed. Gavin might have once been interested in her—really, how could anyone tell?—but at this point, they were solely platonic.

"So you're warning me?" she asked, trying to sound amused. "Otherwise he'll take me off to his lair and have his way with me?"

"No, just, be careful." Silas's tone was edged in frustration. "I don't want to see you get hurt."

Her heart softened. At least she could understand where Silas was coming from. She patted him on the shoulder, "I will be. I have to go, though. Talk to you later?"

She didn't care if Silas approved of her relationship with Gavin or not. She wanted to help Gavin and Emma, and if there was a way to do it, she'd figure out the way to accomplish just that.

CHAPTER FOUR

After the closet incident, as Gavin had dubbed it, Emma seemed to bounce back to her mostly normal self. She'd admitted to Gavin that she'd been afraid that "the people were coming to get her." When he'd pressed her to explain, she'd clammed up and refused to say any more. She hadn't said anything more about what had happened, and although part of him wanted to understand his daughter, another part was hopeful she could get past this and they could somehow make a normal life for themselves in Heron's Landing.

Now, a few weeks after the *closet incident*, Gavin sat in Emma's second-grade classroom for the semester's parent-teacher conference. Emma's teacher, Mrs. Gentry, was a woman in her late thirties who looked more like she was fifty, mostly because she wore her hair in the tightest bun Gavin had ever seen and wore clothes that were probably older than Gavin himself. Mrs. Gentry had recently divorced, and sometimes Gavin wondered if she hated him on sight for being male.

Really, he couldn't blame her. Apparently her husband had cheated on her with his much-younger secretary and subsequently run off to Hawaii, secretary and divorce papers in tow. Mrs. Gentry hadn't changed her name back, though, and it created an odd contrast with the woman sitting in front of him: uptight and stiff and prickly, yet with the salutation of a woman who wanted everyone to acknowledge that she was, in fact, connected to a man.

"Mr. Danvers," she said, shuffling through her papers. "Thank you for coming in. I know a lot of parents don't love these conferences, but I find them hugely beneficial to make certain we are all on the same page as educators and parents. First off, do you have any questions or concerns for me?"

He wanted to ask if this woman understood that Emma was a child to be treated with both delicacy and care, and he wanted to know if she could be that person for his daughter. He wanted to ask how the school had managed to lose his daughter, only for her to be discovered in a closet by a teacher who was only passing by. He wanted to know if he'd ever get his daughter back from wherever she'd disappeared to.

"How is Emma doing?" he asked instead.

Mrs. Gentry pursed her thin lips. "Let me assure you that Emma is a bright child, and she's at the level she should be in all subjects, although she seems to excel most at reading and the language arts. I will say, I've had to tell her to put a book away during class. I applaud her interest in reading, but she needs to understand there's a time and a place for reading, as well."

He almost smiled at this. Emma reminded him of himself in that regard: always cracking open a book instead of listening to a teacher drone on and on. He'd gotten so many demerits and detentions when he'd been caught with a book during class hours; he'd always wanted to say that if teachers didn't want students reading, they shouldn't make class so painfully boring.

"I'll let Emma know that reading shouldn't be done when the teacher is talking. That being said," he couldn't help but add, "I don't want to discourage her from reading in general."

Mrs. Gentry scribbled a note on the paper in front of her. "Certainly not. I know how much of a struggle it can be to get kids to read these days, especially with phones and the Internet and TV distracting them. Books are boring, they tell me. It's a pleasure to see Emma remaining interested in reading."

Gavin sensed a *but* to that sentence. He glanced up to look at the banner above the whiteboard, which read *Celebrate each other!* in bold font. There were other art projects pinned to the walls, from self-portraits to various other kinds of drawings of animals, people, and—was that a tractor? Mrs. Gentry's classroom was decorated in bright primary colors, at odds with the neutral-colored clothes she wore, her hair a similarly neutral ash brown.

But all that dissipated when she tapped her pen against the desk, like she was trying to figure out how to give him some kind of bad news. He almost sighed. Why was it always bad news? For once, he wanted to talk to someone and have them only say, "Everything's great! Don't worry about anything."

"As I've mentioned, Emma is clearly an intelligent child. But her shyness means she has few, if any, friends. I rarely see her playing with other children; on the playground, she's usually by herself reading a book. I hoped that as the school year continued, she would warm up to her classmates, but nothing much has changed. I conferred with Ms. McMurry, and she confirms that Emma acted similarly when she was in her class. And now the incident a few weeks ago, and her behavior lately…" Mrs. Gentry pushed her glasses up her long, thin nose. "I must admit that, overall, I find Emma to be a rather odd child."

Gavin gritted his teeth so hard that his jaw ached. He knew Emma had issues, but Jesus Christ, did her own teacher have to single her out like this?

"She's shy," he replied, his voice surprisingly calm despite his desire to throttle the woman in front of him. "She's had a difficult year. We both have. I think that gives you a reason to have sympathy for her instead of insulting her."

Mrs. Gentry raised meticulously plucked eyebrows. "I apologize if I gave any offense. I merely meant that she's unlike most other children. I wonder if you might consider outside assistance with her?"

"Which means what, exactly?"

"A counselor or therapist. Perhaps someone who could unravel why she's acting like this. I'm a teacher, Mr. Danvers, but I don't have the answers to everything. I'm just afraid that if she isn't able to form friendships now, she'll struggle even more as she gets older. It's hard to be friendless when you're young."

Gavin clenched his fists next to his thigh, trying to rein in his angry responses. He wanted to punch a hole in the wall, or maybe tell Mrs. Gentry to go to hell. He wanted to wrap Emma in cotton and carry her away and keep her from people who thought it would be easier to dismiss a child as odd than try to understand why she preferred to spend time by herself.

"I appreciate your concern, but I've already taken Emma to

more than one therapist. It only made the situation worse." He swallowed, his throat dry. "I've found that keeping her home with me is the best solution right now."

His conversation with Mrs. Gentry continued until finally she requested that he ask the next set of parents to enter. She'd asked about Emma's mother, which Gavin wanted to talk even less about than he wanted to talk about his daughter being odd, and all in all, he rather wished he'd skipped this meeting entirely. But maybe Mrs. Gentry had a point. Maybe Emma was too strange for her age, too out of sorts. What did he know? Sometimes he felt like he didn't know what was up and what was down anymore.

He'd dropped Emma off at his parents' place for the evening. Luckily, his sister Grace planned to be there and could keep Emma company. Emma liked Grace more than she liked most people, and for that, Gavin was infinitely thankful.

A door opened down the hallway, and Kat Williamson stepped out. He froze. He hadn't seen her since she'd told him about Emma hiding in the closet, and for some reason, he felt embarrassed at seeing her again.

Maybe it was because his family seemed bent on making her life more difficult. Kat and Gavin's sister Grace had gotten close a year ago when Kat had helped Grace exonerate her boyfriend Jaime, after he'd been falsely accused of stealing from River's Bend. Now, Kat was the one to discover his daughter hiding in school supply closets.

"Gavin," she said as she approached. "How are you?"

"Fine. Well, not really. But it will be fine, eventually." He knew he was babbling. He ran a hand through his hair. "I don't want to keep dumping my problems on you, though. You don't deserve it."

She smiled a little. "It's not dumping if I want to know, though."

"Still."

They stared at each other, and eventually she gestured to go outside to the parking lot. "I was about to leave anyway. I don't have much in the way of conferences since I'm not a teacher-teacher. If you know what I mean," she said.

"So you're a fake teacher?"

"Ha, something like that. Since I only do one subject, I'm kind of considered to be on the sidelines most days. At any rate, it means I don't have to get yelled at by parents every semester, so I'm not complaining." She stopped in front of a green compact car.

"I want to yell at Emma's teacher," Gavin admitted. He leaned up against her car, and she did the same. She waited. He knew he probably shouldn't talk about one of her colleagues like this, but he was tired and at this point, he didn't care. "She basically said that Emma was odd and needed to see a therapist."

She raised her eyebrows. "Did she really use the word *odd*?"

"Yes."

"Damn. That's unfortunate."

"It seems like such a stupid thing to get angry over. But I keep hearing that word and my blood boils. Like Emma's too *odd* to understand. Who calls a student odd?" He looked at Kat. "Am I overreacting? Please tell me if I am."

Kat hesitated. "I'm not a parent," she finally said slowly, measuring her words. "So I can't say what is and isn't overreacting. That being said, she could've phrased things much better than she did."

He closed his eyes, sighing. "Okay, enough about me. Tell me about your problems."

She let out a sudden laugh. "My problems? You don't want to hear about my problems."

"Yes, I do. If you want to tell me. Mostly I don't want to make this always so uneven between us: me complaining and you having to stand there and listen."

"Didn't I already say that I asked for it?"

"Sure, but sometimes we do things that aren't good for us." She gave him a look, which made him smile for the first time in a while. "Come on, spill it, Williamson."

She stared at him for a moment, like she wasn't sure how to take this request. But before she could speak, her phone rang in her purse. "One sec…" she said as she pulled out her phone. As she read whatever had come in, she made a face before swearing underneath her breath.

Now it was Gavin's turn to raise his eyebrows. "Okay, what was that about?"

"Nothing."

She said it too quickly. He turned so he was facing her and folded his arms. "Nothing means you look at the text and don't make a face like that. Come on, spill."

She worried her plump lower lip with her teeth, and just like that, desire spilled through him. He wanted to touch that lip himself and capture her mouth with his own. Instead, he reached for her arm, trying to pluck her phone from her grasp. "Come on," he cajoled as she laughed, trying to keep the phone from him. "Tell me, otherwise I'll just keep bugging you."

She tried to pull away, but he only snaked an arm around her waist. Now pressed up against him, he gazed down into her eyes, his heart beating fast. He wondered if he should kiss her. His entire body thrilled at the thought.

But then a car horn sounded, and they jumped apart like two teenagers caught necking in the back of a car.

Gavin took a deep breath. What the hell was he doing?

"It wasn't a text message," she blurted.

He just looked at her.

"It was an email, from online. Um, I'm not explaining this well." She rubbed her arms, like she was cold. "Anyway, I keep getting stupid comments on something I put up online, that's all. This was just another one. I need to turn off notifications."

"I don't understand."

She sighed. "Did you know I'm a computer programmer? No? Well, I am. I also recently started making video games. Just for fun. Anyway, I launched a new game and there are some people who aren't happy about it."

Gavin waited for her to explain further, but she didn't seem like she wanted to. "Okay, so what kind of comments? 'This game sucks'? Like that?"

"I wish."

Her voice seemed so sad that his heart clenched. "Kat," he said in a soft voice, "tell me."

To his surprise, she plucked her phone from her purse and, after unlocking it, launched the email in question. "Here, read them yourself."

He wasn't really sure he should be reading her email, but when she gestured at him to take her phone, he gave in. Glancing at the screen, he scrolled through one comment after another, his blood boiling higher with each one.

Girls should be seen and not heard, preferably sitting on my dick, said the first one. Another one read, *Take this down, you fucking copycat.* The comments went on and on, each one worse than the last. By the time he got to the end of the email, he wanted to murder someone.

"These are comments directed at *you?*" he demanded.

She shrugged. "Yeah, or at least the game I made."

"What the hell kind of game is it? Wait, don't answer that. It doesn't matter." He returned her phone. "Can you report these creeps?"

"I do, but they just keep coming back. Anyway, I'll probably just delete the game." She made a face at the suggestion. "Although I hate the thought that they managed to run me off. That almost pisses me off more than the comments themselves."

Gavin marveled at that, both at how Kat managed to stay calm after reading something so insulting, and at how absurd it was that she'd stick it to the man simply to prove that people weren't getting to her. He didn't know whether he wanted to shake her hand or take her by the shoulders and shake some sense into her.

"This isn't right," he told her, trying to make her see that. "I don't know what's going on exactly, but any man who makes those kinds of comments about women should be drawn and quartered by his balls." His earlier anger about Mrs. Gentry's comments regarding Emma only added fuel to his rage now. Could he just find one of these guys and pound them into oblivion? Surely no one would be upset if he did.

Kat smiled. "Thanks, but I'll figure it out. Don't worry about it."

Too late, he thought. *I can't help but worry about you.*

Gazing at her, he thought again how pretty she was. It was rather shallow of him, but he couldn't help it. Everything about her called to some primitive part of him—okay, it was the part of him that wanted to get laid—but there was something else about her that made him want to protect her. Not exactly the way he wanted to protect Emma, but perhaps it was similar. He wanted to carry her away to his tower, keep her safe from everything, and then kiss her until she melted and he could make her his.

But Kat Williamson was convinced she wasn't the type of girl guys needed to save. Gavin rather wanted to prove her wrong anyway.

"I should get going," he said into the night air. "You okay driving home?"

"Why, because some guy will jump me?" At his expression, she patted him on the chest. "Relax. Nothing's going to happen. People are assholes on the Internet all the time. You would know that if you ever used a computer."

The imprint of her hand on his chest made his heart pound. He wanted to curl his hand around her fingers and pull her close. He wished he'd kissed her earlier.

"I use computers, enough to know that you're a smart-ass."

She grinned. "You didn't need a computer to know that."

He growled, her hand still on his chest, and he covered it with his own, pressing her hand against his heart. *Can you feel how fast it beats for you?* he wanted to ask her.

Her eyes widened at the gesture. "Gavin," she whispered.

He wished he'd kissed her earlier? Well, he'd rectify that now. Leaning toward her, he kissed her, and for a moment, she didn't respond. Anxiety filled him. He was about to pull away and apologize when she finally clutched at his shirtfront and kissed him back, and he groaned. He groaned at how soft her lips were and how she tasted like fruit—strawberries?

Cherries? He didn't know and he didn't care. The kiss quickly transformed into something desperate, and when he tangled his tongue with hers, she listed toward him, like she couldn't keep her balance.

Even though she tasted as sweet as could be, he knew he couldn't let this happen again. He was too damaged, too messed up from his divorce to enter into a relationship right now. Kat deserved a guy who could be there for her, not just in spurts and starts. He reluctantly broke the kiss, stroking her cheek with the backs of his fingers.

"I should go," he murmured.

She blinked. "Okay."

He touched her one last time because he just couldn't help himself, and then he left, telling himself that was the last time he'd touch Kat Williamson like that ever again.

CHAPTER FIVE

When are you coming back to LA?

Kat stared at the Facebook message in her inbox and sighed. She wished she had an answer to that particular question, but at the moment, she had no idea. Would she go back to LA at all? It would make sense. She had come to Heron's Landing to care for her grandmother, but now that Lillian had passed away, she was just kind of hanging around, perpetually in limbo.

I'm not sure. But I'll let you know, she wrote, hitting enter before she could rethink her response to her ex-boyfriend's question. She and Marcus had dated for close to three years while she'd attended UCLA and then worked as a computer programmer. Their breakup hadn't been messy or bitter; in fact, it had been a mutual decision. She was moving to Missouri, he wasn't, neither wanted to do long distance. So they'd parted ways and that was that.

Kat sighed again. Was that her life, then? To be logical, practical, but without passion or any real emotion? Her list of boyfriends wasn't extensive, sure, but none of them had made her feel anything beyond a low-level kind of love. The kind of love that only snagged at your heart; the kind of love that didn't burn you if it ended. Instead, you were left empty, wondering if you'd been in love in the first place.

Kat shook herself. Now she was getting ridiculous over a one-off Facebook message. Marcus hadn't been the love of her life. So what? Maybe she wasn't cut out for such a thing. Maybe it was a myth.

Then again, thinking about Gavin Danvers, she had a feeling it wasn't a myth. The way he'd kissed her had been nothing like any of the kisses she'd received from other men. His kisses had made her *yearn*. Not just for sex—but that was there, too—but to wrap herself in him. To meld herself to him and never let go.

It was both strange and terrifying. Getting off the couch, she went to the kitchen to make some tea, mostly for something to do. But even as the kettle boiled and she placed the teabag in her mug, she thought about that kiss. She thought about the look on Gavin's face, and how he'd looked at her with desire and something like resignation. She had a distinct feeling that any kind of relationship with a man like him wouldn't be uncomplicated or low-level. It would sear her to her very soul.

As the evening waned on, Kat found herself looking at the page where she still hosted her contentious video game. The comments rolled in, and for the most part, she avoided reading them now. She'd considered taking the game down, but the very stubborn part of her refused to give in. Why should she be scared of a bunch of Internet trolls who probably lived in their mothers' basements and hated women simply for existing? She wasn't going to apologize for posting a game making fun of men like that. At any rate, she was getting enough revenue in ad money that pulling the plug didn't make sense. She'd collect her money from these guys' tears and laugh all the way to the bank.

She was about to close her laptop for the night when an email popped into her inbox. Seeing the subject—READ IMMEDIATELY—she had a feeling it was spam. She was about to delete it, but curiosity got the better of her. It always did.

To Whom It May Concern:

Fuck you BITCH. I'll find out where you live and then you'll be sorry.

Kat stared at the email, breathing harder. She read the words over and over again and her heart pounded so hard she felt dizzy. Slapping her laptop shut, she fought tears. It was one thing to get insulting comments via email; it was another entirely to be receiving threats.

She crawled into bed, but not without getting a knife from the kitchen to hide underneath her pillow for the entirety of the night.

The weekend dawned bright and gorgeous, with autumn edging the leaves with oranges and yellows. After much deliberation, Kat decided to delete the game, but she had a feeling it was too late. She knew as well as anyone that nothing on the Internet could ever be completely deleted. Hoping that it would deter some of the lazier trolls, though, she heaved a sigh and deleted it, making certain to leave as little a trail as she could manage.

She refused to let that email ruin her weekend. She walked to Trudy's, which was the one café in the tiny downtown of Heron's Landing. Main Street was barely a street, but it hosted Heron's Landing's various shops: a general store with apartments above it; Trudy's café; a hardware store; a craft shop that exploded with Christmas paraphernalia, usually by October 1. Today, there were quite a few tourists wandering the street. Heron's Landing felt like it was stuck in time, and after touring the vineyard, many tourists came downtown to experience the town's particular type of charm. Kat smiled as she watched an older couple trying to take a selfie in front of a huge elm tree. As she passed by, they waved at her, and she became their photographer for a few moments.

"Thank you, miss," the older man said as she handed back his phone. "Still can't figure out these new phones. Give me a rotary phone any day of the week, I say."

His wife snorted. "You couldn't dial my number right on any rotary phone, Ernest! Honestly, he's been useless with technology since he was born."

Ernest's eyes twinkled as he looked at his wife. "And yet you still married me."

Kat walked on, hands in her pockets. Seeing that couple reminded her that love could be stronger than what she'd seen personally. Her own parents had divorced when she was a young girl, and Kat had stayed with her mother until she'd passed away from breast cancer. She'd always been a bit of a loner. Maybe it wasn't *love* that was the problem: maybe it was her.

"Kat!" Kat looked up to see Grace Danvers moving toward her, a bright smile on her face. "I haven't seen you in ages! How are you?"

Grace was a pretty, young woman, recently turned twenty-four, and her once-long blonde hair was now in a bob that reached right below her chin. Despite her stylish haircut, though, she still wore her usual skirts and peasant tops, a smudge of flour on her cheek.

Kat hugged her close. "It has been too long," she admitted as she sat down at a nearby booth. "How are you, though?"

Grace beamed. She thrust out her hand, and Kat couldn't help but gasp as she saw the ring sparkling on her finger.

"Oh, Grace," she said, gazing at the bright sapphire ring. "It's gorgeous. When did Jaime ask you?"

"Just yesterday. I had no idea he was going to do it, the jerk. I was so surprised I couldn't think of anything to say, and he just about had a heart attack." Grace handed Kat a menu. "I mean, we'd talked about getting engaged, but I didn't expect it to happen for a while yet."

"I'm so happy for you." And Kat was, although her heart squeezed with a bite of jealousy all the same. She'd seen how Grace and Jaime had almost lost each other, and seeing them happy and in love now made her glad that she'd helped them in a small way. After Jaime had been accused of stealing from the vineyard, Kat had assisted Grace with discovering—and finding real evidence of—the actual culprit. And now the two of them would be getting married.

"But what about you?" Grace asked, scooting into the seat opposite her. At Kat's look, Grace waved a hand. "No one's around, and Trudy's in the kitchen."

Kat hesitated. She couldn't very well tell Grace about kissing her brother, could she? And she didn't want to talk about the game or the emails. "Everything's good. Just been working, you know. The daily grind."

"You still like teaching?"

"For the most part. Sometimes it can be difficult, but the

kids are sweet. I think it helps that I'm not teaching middle school or high school. Teenagers are kind of terrifying."

Grace smiled. "Seriously. I remember what I was like at thirteen and shudder."

"I think we all do." Kat shrugged, not sure what else to tell Grace. "Otherwise it's been pretty uneventful."

Okay, that was a lie. A big ole fat lie.

Grace traced something on the table. "I heard about Emma, about what you did," she said quietly. "I hope you know how grateful we all are. I know Gavin can't thank you enough."

A flush of pleasure filled Kat. "It wasn't anything, really. I did what anyone else would do." She bit the inside of her cheek now, wondering if she was overstepping her bounds. But Grace was more…receptive than the other members of the Danvers family. "Is Emma…do you know what's going on? She's quiet and shy as usual in my class. Almost too quiet, if I'm being honest."

Grace let out a long sigh. "I wish I could tell you, but Gavin is so protective of her, even when it comes to the rest of the family. I saw her yesterday, and she seemed like you described her. But I still worry. About them both. They've gone through so much…" She rubbed her forehead, suddenly looking older than twenty-four. "I just hope they can figure things out, you know?"

Kat did know. She'd thought about Emma ever since she'd discovered her in that closet, and more and more, she wondered if the girl had some kind of illness that couldn't just be classified as being homesick or missing her mother. Kat wasn't an expert, and she wasn't a psychiatrist, but she'd dealt with anxiety and had a panic attack more than once in her life, and she couldn't help but think Emma was suffering something similar.

"Has Gavin taken her to anyone?" Kat couldn't help but ask.

"Not recently, no. He and Emma had a bad experience with a therapist last year, and I think it's scared my brother away since."

Someone called Grace's name, and the girl popped up out of the booth like a jack-in-the-box. "Gotta run. But Kat," she said as she touched her arm, "I feel like if anyone could get through to my brother, it would be you."

Kat's eyebrows rose to her hairline. "Me?"

"Yes, you. I may be a bit of an airhead, but I've seen the way he looks at you. Kat, he's *smiled* at you. He doesn't smile at anyone. Well, except Emma, although not as much recently since he's been so worried about her."

"I don't think I'm the best person…" Kat trailed off, not sure how to explain.

"Just, don't take my brother's aloofness as him not caring, okay? He's a hard nut to crack, but I swear, when you do crack it, it'll be worth it." Someone called Grace's name again, and she called back an "I'm coming!" before snagging the menu and running into the back, leaving Kat to try to figure out how she felt about all this.

In times of emotional distress, Kat generally preferred to lay things out in a logical order. She was a computer programmer; everything in life had its own kind of code, she reasoned. She snagged a piece of paper from her purse and began scribbling on it.

What I do know, she wrote at the top.

- *I'm attracted to Gavin*
- *Proof: I want(ed) him to kiss me*
- *He's attracted to me.*
- *Proof: He want(ed) to kiss me*
- *I like him as a person*
- *Proof: I like talking to him. I want to know more about him. I can't stop thinking about him, etc.*
- *He likes me as a person.*
- *Proof: He likes talking to me (debatable: he doesn't talk much in general). He wants to know more about me (debatable: he hasn't said as much but listens when I talk about myself). He can't stop thinking about me (no idea: he could forget about me most of the time.)*
- *I would like a relationship with him.*
- *Proof: see above.*
- *He would like a relationship with me.*
- *Proof: ????*

"Hey, I never got your order," Grace said at her shoulder.

Kat grabbed the piece of paper and shoved it into her purse, extremely glad that it was difficult to see a blush on her dark skin. Because she was most definitely blushing—and feeling like a complete idiot.

"Um, coffee is fine," she finally stammered.

"Coming right up. You like cream, right?"

Kat nodded as Grace walked away, trying to steady her breathing. She really shouldn't list personal things like that in the middle of a busy café. Did she *want* to be found out?

She finished her coffee in record speed, suddenly feeling like the walls at Trudy's were closing in on her. She needed some fresh air. She needed to get Grace's words out of her head. And she most definitely needed to stop thinking about Gavin Danvers and how he felt about her, because God only knew if the man was capable of any kind of deeper feelings.

But as luck would have it, she wasn't going to get to stop thinking about the man of the hour that easily. Just as she was leaving Trudy's, she saw him and Emma walking in her very direction. When he saw her, he seemed taken aback, like he was surprised to see her in this very town. She almost snorted. Did he really think he wasn't going to run into her in a town of fewer than three hundred people?

"Hi, Mr. Danvers, hi, Emma," she said with a small wave. "How are you?"

Emma had her hair up in what Kat thought was supposed to be braids, but she wasn't entirely sure. After Gavin had greeted her in his usual gruff way, Emma opened her mouth like she was about to say something, but then thought better of it.

"How's your weekend been, Emma?" Kat asked, ignoring her frustrating father.

"Okay," the girl murmured. But then her eyes lit up as she added, "We found some kittens at the back of Mike's. There are *five* of them. All black."

"Oh my. I love kittens. You'll have to show me. Is the mom black, too?"

Emma nodded. "Dad says they're probably four weeks old. They still have blue eyes, too. Did you know cats' eyes change as they get older?"

Kat glanced at Gavin. He shrugged, like he didn't know who this chatterbox of a girl was in front of them.

"I think I did know that. I had a black cat when I was a kid. Her name was Snowball."

Emma frowned. "That doesn't make sense."

"I know, but I didn't name her. We got her from the pound, and she didn't respond to any other name."

"Come on, Emma. I'm sure Ms. Williamson needs to get home," Gavin said.

"No, not really. I'm just taking a walk." Kat glanced at Gavin, but he was making a studied effort not to look at her. *Lovely. Now he's just going to act like we never kissed? This day keeps getting better.*

Seeing that Gavin didn't seem all that interested in continuing to chat, Kat added, "I'll see you later, then. Maybe I'll come by to see those kittens, okay?"

She pulled out her phone as Gavin and Emma walked in the direction of the café. It had become a habit, checking her email and her messages if she found herself wandering around alone. Marcus hadn't replied yet, for which she was rather grateful. But as she perused her email, she noticed that she'd gotten another message from what seemed like the person who'd threatened her the day before, although the email address was different.

"Son of a bitch," she muttered under her breath. Then fear congealed in her gut when she saw that this email was accompanied by a drawing that involved a man shooting a woman as she sat at her computer. Everything around her faded away, until all she saw was that stupid drawing, probably made in Paint. But her heart pounded all the same.

"Everything okay?"

She whirled to see that Gavin hadn't gone inside Trudy's yet. "Why are you still here?" she blurted. She almost laughed at his expression. "Sorry, that was rude. Everything's fine." She tried very hard to make her voice even, but she could hear it waver.

Apparently, so could he. "Really? Because once again I find you swearing at your phone, and you look like you've seen a ghost. Is it the same thing you got last time?"

Kat was about to lie and say it wasn't, but she knew Gavin could probably see past any pretense. Emma was looking at them both, her forehead crinkled in confusion.

"Yeah, same thing. It's just annoying, like I said. Don't worry about it." She put her phone back into her purse, but she realized she was shaking so badly that she almost dropped it. Dammit, now was not the time to lose it.

Gavin stepped closer to her, touching her on the arm. "You don't look all right," he said in a quiet voice. "Tell me what's happened. Let me help you."

"What's happened?" Emma asked. "Are you okay, Ms. Williamson?"

Kat swallowed back the fear. "I'm okay. Just a little unsettled. I didn't get some good news."

"Emma, why don't you go inside Trudy's and find Grace? I'll be in in a sec." Gavin watched his daughter enter the café before turning to Kat. "Now tell me what happened."

Once again Kat found herself handing over her phone, but this time, she wasn't embarrassed. For some reason, having Gavin know about what was happening allowed her to calm down somewhat. She could breathe again. And seeing his thunderous expression when he saw the email? She knew he'd do anything in his power to keep her safe.

That was something she'd never experienced before.

"What the ever-loving fuck?" He swore some more, grinding his teeth until Kat was sure he'd have only dust for teeth in a moment. "This is not okay. We have to go to the police."

"I don't disagree, but what are they going to do? I know this person—or persons—is untraceable. It's a threat, but unless they can ID him, the most I could do is get a restraining order, if I knew who he was. But since we don't, there's not much we can do."

Gavin just glared at the ground. "I get what you're saying," he finally said, "but I'm not going to sit around and do nothing." He took her hands. "I'm not going to let anyone hurt you, Kat. I promise you that. I don't know what I'm going to do, but we need to figure this out. Can you come over tonight?"

She blinked. "To your apartment?"

At that, his fierce expression softened into a grin. "For dinner only. I promise. Emma will be there anyway."

She still hesitated. Being in Gavin's space, seeing his apartment, just being in close quarters? It was a recipe for disaster. Or rather, a recipe for letting whatever this was get beyond a few kisses in a parking lot one night.

But Kat realized with a start that she didn't want to return to her grandmother's house all alone to think and stew and be afraid.

"Okay, yes. Dinner. Should I bring anything?"

He smiled, and her heart pounded for an entirely different reason now. "Just yourself. I'll take care of the rest."

CHAPTER SIX

"Emma, could you set the table?" Gavin called from the kitchen.

He could see his daughter's blonde head pop up from the couch before she called back, "What?"

He sighed. "Come set the table, please!"

"Why? We never set the table for dinner."

God save him from questioning eight-year-olds. Although Emma was shy around people she didn't know and was often extremely self-conscious in public, she managed to seem more like your usual kid when at home. It was some small comfort to Gavin that the daughter he'd gotten used to before everything that had happened still existed.

Emma wandered into the kitchen to watch him. "What are you doing?"

"What does it look like I'm doing?"

"You're cooking." Her eyes narrowed. "Why?"

"Ms. Williamson is coming to dinner, that's why. Now, go set the table like I asked you to."

Emma rolled her eyes, but Gavin was so happy to see her

acting like a real kid that he didn't have the heart to reprimand her for it. Better to have a daughter rolling her eyes than hiding behind him because she was terrified of invisible monsters.

He heard the clatter of silverware and glasses as he attempted to finish sautéing the vegetables. After messaging Jaime for advice on what to serve, Gavin had decided a quiche would be easiest to manage in the short time frame he'd given himself. When he'd asked Kat for dinner, he'd realized—only afterward—that he'd have to, in fact, cook something edible. Most nights he was too tired to do more than put something in the oven or microwave for himself and Emma. He winced inwardly. He probably should do better on that front, at least for Emma, if not for himself.

"Okay, I'm done," Emma said as she came back into the tiny kitchen. They currently lived in a small apartment above Mike's grocery store, and although it had two bedrooms, sometimes it felt overly crowded with one adult and one child. It was a far cry from their house in Boston. Then again, that house had too many painful memories; it was the last place Gavin wanted to return to.

"Did you use placemats?" he asked absently, wondering if the zucchini was supposed to be this soft.

Emma made a huffing sound. "Of course I did."

"Good. Be sure to fill a pitcher with ice water before Kat— I mean Ms. Williamson—gets here."

She didn't say anything, but just watched as he transferred the vegetables to a plate. Gavin hadn't taken much in the way of stuff when he'd left Boston. All the china and silverware he hadn't cared anything about. Now, though, he wished he had something nicer than plastic plates and glasses. How he'd ended up bringing any placemats with him was beyond him. He'd been in such a daze it was a wonder he'd managed to get himself all the way here without incident.

A knock on the front door sounded, and Emma ran to get it before Gavin even asked her to. He listened as Kat said hello to Emma, and he tried to stop his heart from racing as he thought about Kat being here, in his apartment, which was only a few yards from his bedroom, which had his bed, which he could kiss her in, and touch her, and…

"It smells amazing," Kat said as she walked into the kitchen. "You cooked for me?"

Gavin opened the oven to take out the quiche. He sighed in relief to see it wasn't a soupy mess, but it still needed a few more minutes. "I tried, at least," he replied grimly. "If it tastes awful, feel free to tell me as much."

"Don't worry, we will," Emma chirped.

He gave Emma a look. "How about you go show Ms. Williamson those kittens, little miss sassy?"

Emma didn't need to be asked twice. She practically bolted from the apartment, dragging Kat along with her. Knowing Emma, she'd knock on Joy McGuire's door—Gavin's brother's fiancée—and ask her to come, too, even though she'd seen the kittens at least twice already.

Gavin had a feeling Emma would ask to keep one of those kittens, but they were still too young to part from their mother, so he had a bit of time to stall. He wasn't averse to having a pet, but right now he had way too much on his plate to care for a kitten. Emma could help, but she was young enough that Gavin would still have to help her.

He rubbed the back of his neck. He didn't need to be thinking about kittens right now. He needed to figure out how to help Kat with these threats she'd received. Gavin didn't know anything about Internet trolls and gamers and whatever else Kat had talked about, but he did know cowards, and he refused to see Kat scared and upset again. Not if he could prevent it.

The timer dinged for the quiche, and he opened the oven to pull it out. After placing the quiche and vegetables on the table, he grabbed the loaf of bread he'd picked up from the store and hoped that the meal was at least decent. He wasn't a bad cook, per se, just an inexperienced one. When he'd been married and Teagan had been well, she'd usually cooked for the family. After she'd started spiraling, though, meals had become less and less important. It had become more about surviving, if he was honest.

The front door opened as the pair returned. "Dad, one of the kittens has a white spot on its belly!" Emma gave him the news like she'd discovered the cure for cancer, and he couldn't help but smile. "And I think one of them is going to be long-haired while the rest are short-haired."

"Interesting. Go wash your hands before dinner," Gavin replied. He looked up to see Kat smiling. She'd changed since he'd seen her earlier, wearing tight skinny jeans with boots and a bright red blouse. When she smiled, though, it transformed her face, and she became not merely pretty, but beautiful. And when she turned and showed off that amazing ass of hers? Gavin had to stifle a groan.

This really hadn't been his best idea, he admitted to himself.

Kat washed her hands before they all sat down for dinner. Despite her loquaciousness just moments earlier, Emma reverted to her normally shy self now with Kat sitting at the table. Gavin had a feeling it was because the excitement over showing Kat the kittens had faded, and now his daughter preferred to keep quiet. It didn't help that Gavin found himself tongue-tied. Could he ever figure out how to act around this woman?

"The quiche is very good," Kat offered into the silence. She didn't seem fazed by the silence, and he admired her ability to talk to people with ease. "Thanks again for inviting me," she added.

Gavin nodded. "You're welcome."

He wanted to ask her about the emails, but it wasn't exactly a subject you discussed over dinner. Finally, he landed on the mundane. "How's work?"

"Much the same as always. I teach the kids about computers and hope they don't forget everything the next day." Kat picked up her wineglass and swirled the wine before sipping it. "Some days a student will press the print button twenty times and we end up with some huge photo printed over and over again, so that's usually exciting."

His mouth twitched. He looked at Emma, but she was studiously gazing at her plate. Perhaps talking about school and students wasn't the best idea around a girl who was one of her students.

He fell silent, feeling awkward and stupid. He'd only had one girlfriend—and then that girlfriend had become his wife—and so he had little experience with women. Having a daughter helped in a way, but he didn't really know how to talk to a woman as put-together and beautiful and smart as Kat. She radiated confidence. Even as she cut into her piece of quiche, she somehow managed to do so with style. Gavin couldn't explain it.

"So you were living in Boston?" Kat asked.

"Yes. For about six years or so."

"Is Emma's mom still there?"

Gavin swallowed. He glanced at Emma, who was now slumping down into her chair like she was trying to disappear.

"Yes, she is." Gavin knew he sounded tight-lipped and borderline rude, but the last thing he wanted to talk about was Teagan. He wished he could talk about his ex-wife without feeling like the weight of the world was on his shoulders, but at the moment, thinking about her only reminded him of how he'd failed his family completely.

I couldn't save her. And now I'm afraid I won't be able to help my daughter, either.

Kat, as if realizing she'd ventured into awkward territory, seemed to decide that silence was her best option. Gavin didn't know what to say either, so the dinner continued with only the sounds of silverware against plates and water glasses being lifted. When Emma asked to be excused after eating only a few bites, he didn't have the energy to fight her.

Emma went to her room, closing the door. Gavin knew she was retreating into her books, which he understood completely. He had always done the same. Although recently he'd had less time to read, he remembered reading book after book as a kid just like Emma did now. Books couldn't hurt you—not really. A book could surprise you, sadden you, anger you, but when you closed it, it was over. It had never happened. The fantasy would dissipate, and soon you'd be thrust back into cold reality, the glimmers of that fantasy slowly fading.

Despite his insistence otherwise, Kat helped with the

dishes. Gavin could barely concentrate on washing anything with her standing next to him, so close he could smell her perfume. She smelled spicy yet sweet, and he wanted to inhale against her skin to take in all the notes. How did she manage to unsettle him just by standing next to him?

They retreated to the living room, where one wall was covered with books of all sorts. Gavin might not have taken any of the china, but he'd made certain to bring his books. A wineglass in hand, Kat perused the shelves, touching some of the spines with light brushes of her fingers.

"Do you have a favorite?" she asked.

"I don't, actually. I know I should, but I could never decide."

He saw her try to hide a smile. "Then what are some of your favorites?"

"Would it be cheesy to say that all of these are?"

She pulled out a copy of *One Hundred Years of Solitude*. "You've read all these? Impressive. I don't know if I've read thirty percent of the books on my shelf."

"I only keep the ones I like. I have a rule that if I don't read a book within a year of buying it, I donate it."

She laughed. "If I had that rule, I wouldn't have any books left." Placing the book in her hand back onto the shelf, she continued looking before taking out another one. "*Lady Chatterley's Lover*, huh? I have read this one."

Gavin felt a blush on his cheeks, and then wanted to blush for blushing. "It's a good book," he said in a hoarse voice.

Kat shrugged. "I don't know. I wasn't much for the guy—what's his name? Mellors?—mansplaining all over the place. Telling Connie how she should orgasm and everything."

Gavin coughed on the wine he was drinking, and Kat

good-naturedly hit him on the back. He waved her away, and she just laughed. "That's not exactly how I read the book," he replied, "but why am I not surprised by you saying something like that?"

"What's that supposed to mean?" She put her hands on her hips, although the smile on her face belied her irritation.

"Just that you're so…" He struggled to find the right word. "Forthright. You aren't afraid to say what you mean."

"You mean I'm too opinionated and should keep it to myself."

He shook his head. "The opposite. I wish more people were like you. Hell, I wish *I* were more like you. I think too much about what other people think about me."

She didn't say anything, simply sipping her wine thoughtfully. He gazed at her profile, taking in the slope of her nose, her full lips, the dimples in her cheeks. Her skin shimmered in the low light, and he remembered touching her that night in the parking lot. How she'd been soft as silk and tasted like strawberries.

"I think that's the first time someone's said they wanted to be like me," she admitted. "Most of my life, people have told me that I shouldn't be so opinionated. Flamboyant. Talkative. I never to get to just be a woman who has things to say and maybe isn't quiet about it." She shrugged, flicking her gaze to him. "But now I'm just talking about nothing."

"Nothing you could say would mean nothing to me," he admitted.

She smiled. "Even though that made no sense, I'm going to say thank you anyway."

He bowed, which just made her laugh. Had he ever heard

her laugh before? It was a sound he could listen to all day, every day.

He didn't know if was the quiet of the apartment, or how she looked standing next to him, or if it was just a quirk of fate that he could not control, but as she turned toward him, he said in a voice he barely recognized, "I'm going to kiss you."

Her eyes widened. She wasn't laughing now, for which he was patently grateful. But to his surprise, she wrapped her arms around his neck and said, "Oh thank God," before she ended up kissing *him.*

It was like a match to a wick. They inflamed each other, and Gavin pulled her close so that their bodies aligned, her softness to his hardness. She was taller than Teagan was, and he had to admit, it was nice not to get a crick in his neck from kissing. All thoughts of his ex-wife fluttered away, though, when she slicked her tongue inside his mouth. He groaned, his hand sliding down her back to cup her ass. He felt her inhalation of breath.

The kiss lengthened, became something neither of them expected. It was sweet and desperate, all tongues and teeth, soft moans and groans filling the space between them. He wanted to touch her everywhere, and his hands didn't stay in one spot for long. Her ass, her back, her shoulders, her arms. He wanted to strip her bare and revel in her body.

Kat was no passive partner. She kissed him with equal fervor, and when he felt her hands sliding up under his shirt, he practically jumped out of his skin with want. *Yes, touch me, feel me,* he thought frantically. Gliding her fingers up his abdomen, she circled his belly button before going higher. She flicked one of his flat nipples, and for that, he nipped at her plush bottom lip.

He'd grown so hard it was almost painful. He wished she'd delve lower, take him in hand, and stroke his cock until he came. As if she read his mind, her other hand teased around the waistband of his jeans.

"Jesus, Kat," he groaned against her mouth.

She just toyed with him, only dancing her fingertips across his skin. She dipped a finger near the button of his jeans, and he almost lost all of his self-control.

"I'd make a joke about you being happy to see me, but that seems kind of unfair right now," she whispered.

He grasped that roving hand and pressed it against his hard cock. She gasped, and he leaned in to kiss her as she fondled him through his jeans.

About to beg her to put her bare hand on him, he stroked the line of her neck when he heard a door creak open. He barely registered the sound, but Kat came to her senses more quickly than he did. She jumped away from him just as Emma came into the living room.

The three of them stared at each other in silence. Gavin tried to control his breathing and turned away so his arousal wouldn't be visible, and he could see Kat trying to put herself together as well. Emma simply blinked at them before walking into the kitchen. Gavin heard her turn on the faucet before she walked back to her room, water glass in hand.

He let out a breath. Kat snorted, and he glared at her.

"I think that's the sign for me to go." She smoothed her clothes, although she looked barely wrinkled. Whereas Gavin felt like he'd been sent through the wringer twenty times over.

"Let me walk you home," he offered.

"No, it's fine. I need the fresh air." She hesitated, but then leaned up to kiss him on the cheek. "Thank you for dinner."

After Kat left, Gavin realized with a start that they hadn't talked about that email she'd gotten. He cursed. What kind of protector was he if he got so distracted by kissing her that he couldn't come up with a way to keep her safe? After his body had calmed down and his mind wasn't quite as filled with thoughts of her in his bed, he sent her a quick text.

Forgot to talk about that email. Still think you should go to the police.

Her reply was almost instantaneous: *That's not what I was thinking about on my walk home, but I'll think about it. Have a good night, Gavin.*

CHAPTER SEVEN

"Ms. Williamson, I think my computer froze."

Kat looked up from her own computer to see Danny Tucker raising his hand. She restrained a sigh. The kid's computer inevitably froze at least twice each class period, mostly because he seemed determined to press as many buttons as possible until the computer gave up the fight.

Kat fiddled with the mouse and, seeing that the cursor was frozen, she used the tried and true Control-Alt-Delete and told Danny to do only exactly as he was told when the computer rebooted. Danny nodded, but she knew that was basically code for "I'm going to mess around again the second your back is turned."

Kat didn't mind teaching most days. The kids were entertaining, and she essentially babysat while they played keyboard games to improve their typing skills. It was a far cry from her work as a computer programmer, and if she thought about how she was wasting her own education to sit here and make sure kids like Danny didn't cause their computers to explode, she might shed a few tears. But at the same time, she had enough to keep her preoccupied and not restless; besides, she'd only lost her grandmother a few months ago. She didn't have the heart to abandon the house yet, and the town Lillian had lived in for decades.

You're always taking care of everyone, Lillian had said more than once before she'd started to slide into a fast decline. *But who's taking care of you? I worry about you, Katherine.*

Kat had always taken care of others, it was true. She'd taken care of her mom, she'd taken care of Lillian. She'd taken care of friends and her exes and she'd taken care of dogs and cats, but more recently, the weight of caretaking had felt almost too heavy to bear. And now she had another person on her mind—or persons, plural.

In the week since she'd kissed Gavin Danvers a second time, she'd barely seen the man. They'd run into each other a few times, but he'd only greeted her in a gruff voice and never stopped to talk. Kat didn't know what to make of him. He invited her to dinner, he kissed her in his living room, he begged her to touch him, and then…nothing. He'd ghosted on her as badly as any guy she'd dated in undergrad. Normally she'd write him off, but with Gavin, she had a feeling there was more to this than him suddenly deciding he was no longer interested.

She'd also seen the look in his eyes when she'd touched him. He wanted her—there was no doubt about that. Desire could only take them so far, but it was at least a start. And if Kat was honest with herself, she'd admit that she was lonely. Not just for sex, but for companionship. Having that person you could talk to after work, that person you got to see as the evening wound down into night. And even that person who could take care of you, just as much as you took care of them.

Feeling restless, she got up from her chair to wander the room, looking over kids' shoulders to see their progress. Given this class consisted only of second graders, most of the students continued to "hunt and peck" their way through typing exercises, despite Kat's corrections and insistence that they use the right fingers for particular keys. Then again, by the time these kids were in college, they'd probably have computer programs that allowed them to avoid typing altogether.

Seeing that Danny was actually typing instead of trying to get online, Kat wandered to the edge of the class, where Emma Danvers sat. Her head was down, her focus on the monitor in front of her, but Kat soon realized the girl wasn't typing. Instead, she seemed almost dazed.

Kat laid a hand on her shoulder. Emma barely responded to the touch. "Emma? Are you all right?"

Emma didn't say anything. Kat watched as the girl's breathing increased, and she squatted down to her level to get a better look at her. Emma's breaths were fast and frantic, and soon the girl started moaning low in her throat.

"Emma, look at me," Kat said in a low voice. "What's wrong?"

By this point, most of the students had stopped typing and were staring at the pair. Emma, though, seemed like she was in her own little world. When she started hyperventilating, though, Kat's heart froze. She caught Emma's gaze. "Emma, I need to get you to calm down. Take a long, deep breath for me? That's it. And let it out. Do that again. Count to ten as you breathe in, and count to ten as you breathe out."

Emma's breaths slowed enough that Kat was able to leave to go to the classroom next door, where she knew Silas was working during his break. When he saw her expression, he didn't even ask what she needed. He got up and followed her back into the lab.

"I'm taking Emma to the nurse," Kat said. "Watch my class for me?"

"Of course. Do you want me to call her dad?" Silas glanced at Emma, whose hand Kat had taken.

"Please, and let Mrs. Gentry know as well." She tugged on Emma's hand. "Let's go to the nurse, okay?"

Emma didn't say anything, but she followed Kat without protest.

"Keep counting and breathing," Kat said as they walked down the deserted hallways. "Good girl. You're okay. Keep breathing just like that."

When they got to the nurse's office, Kat swore under her breath when she saw that the nurse was at lunch. Perfect. What was she supposed to do now? She wasn't exactly a trained medical professional.

She sat Emma down in one of the chairs, kneeling in front of her. She continued counting and making Emma take slow, deep breaths, but as the minutes passed, Kat could tell that Emma's initial calm was disappearing already. Tears filled her eyes and trailed down her pale cheeks. Kat rubbed her hands, murmuring soothing things, desperate to try to keep the girl from panicking.

Emma started wheezing. Kat went searching for a paper bag, something she could use to help Emma, and she snatched a bag from inside one of the cabinets.

"Breathe into this," she instructed as she handed the bag to Emma. "And I'll count for you. Breathe in, one, two, three, four…"

Emma's breath hiccupped with sobs, and it broke Kat's heart. What had terrified Emma so much? She remembered her conversation with Grace at Trudy's, and she wondered once again if Emma wasn't suffering from some kind of anxiety disorder. This couldn't be normal behavior for an eight-year-old, right?

The nurse still hadn't returned, but fortunately, Emma's breathing calmed down. Tears still fell from her eyes, though, and Kat rubbed her hands to soothe her.

"I think I'm dying," Emma said. "I couldn't breathe."

"I know, but you're okay. You'll be okay. I promise."

"I had a dream last night that my mom..." Emma bit her lip. "She was in a car accident. What if she dies? What if I saw what's going to happen to her?"

Kat was at a loss, but she kept saying the same thing over and over again. "Everything's going to be fine. Your mom is okay. You'll be okay."

"I want my dad." Emma pulled her knees up until her face rested against them. "When is he coming?"

"We called him, sweetheart. He'll be here any minute. I promise."

Emma nodded and fell silent. Kat could only hope that meant she'd calmed down somewhat.

After what seemed like hours, Kat heard quick footsteps outside in the hallway, and then Gavin was in the doorway, his face pale and grim. "*Jesus*...Emma." He saw Kat, and he nodded. "Emma, what happened?"

When Emma looked up at her dad, she promptly burst into tears again, sobs wracking her small frame. Kat rose so Gavin could hug his daughter close as she cried.

"I saw Mom die in my dream. I tried to stop thinking

about it like you told me, but I couldn't. Have you talked to her? Are you sure she's okay? I want to call her right now." Emma was almost babbling, and Gavin just stroked her hair.

"We can call your mom after we get you calmed down a little, okay? But she's okay. It was just a dream. Remember when I told you that things in dreams aren't going to come true?"

"But what if *this time* something happens? You don't know something bad won't happen." Emma's lip quivered. "You don't know that for sure."

Gavin seemed at a loss. "Come on, let's get you home."

Right then, the nurse finally arrived, and she seemed confused at seeing all these people in her office. "Goodness, what happened?" she asked.

"I'm taking Emma home. Where are her things?"

"I'll go get them," the nurse offered. "She's in second grade, right? I'll go and talk to Mrs. Gentry real quick."

Kat was infinitely grateful the woman offered, as she wanted to talk to Gavin for a second. She was well aware she wasn't a psychiatrist, but she wondered if Gavin had any idea what was wrong with Emma. During her mother's illness, Kat had suffered from panic attacks from time to time, and she recognized the same symptoms that Emma was suffering from now. She also knew that oftentimes, people who hadn't ever experienced panic attacks didn't realize what they were in other people.

The nurse left, and Kat said, "Can I talk to you a second?"

Gavin rose. "We'll just be over here," he said to Emma as he followed Kat further into the nurse's office.

"What is it?" His voice seemed so sad, so resigned, that Kat wanted to embrace him. She wanted to tell him things would get better, but like Emma had asked, how did she know? She didn't know if things would get better, and she knew that this was a situation she couldn't take care of.

"It's just that, Emma saying she couldn't stop thinking about her mom dying…" Kat struggled to find the words. "I used to be like that. When my mom got cancer, I'd have panic attacks, like I couldn't breathe, and I couldn't stop thinking about how my mom would die and leave me all alone. Sometimes I couldn't go to school, it was so bad." The words left her in a rush, and at Gavin's expression, she wasn't sure he'd caught all of it. "Emma seems to be experiencing the same thing."

"Which is?"

"I think she's suffering from anxiety. I mean, that's obvious. But I mean, I think she may have some kind of anxiety disorder. Maybe even OCD." When Gavin said nothing, Kat swallowed against a suddenly dry throat. But she'd gone this far already. "Have you taken her to someone before? To get her checked out?"

Apparently, that was the wrong thing to say. He scowled, and she almost stepped back at the expression on his face. "You mean take her to a shrink so they can medicate her until she's a zombie?"

Kat blinked. "That's not what I meant, no."

"Look, I know you mean well. You're a good person; I know that. But Emma's not your kid. She's *mine*. And although I appreciate your input, I'm not taking her to another therapist. The last time…" He looked away, a muscle twitching in his jaw. "I've had enough with psychologists and counselors and psychiatrists to last a lifetime."

"I know it's hard to find someone you can trust and who works for you, but you can't give up that easily."

"I can 'give up' as much as I please," he hissed. "You know nothing about this. You don't. Don't try to act like you're providing me with some revelation."

Kat was so startled by his vehemence that she couldn't speak. This wasn't the Gavin she thought she knew: he'd been gruff, and unsociable, but never outright cruel. She struggled against either crying or slapping his face.

"If this is how you react to people trying to help you, no wonder you don't want to work with any professionals."

"I also don't take well to anyone telling me my daughter may be mentally ill." Gavin glanced at Emma, his face softening a fraction. "I've seen mental illness up close, Kat," he said in a voice that broke her heart all over again. "I've seen it, and by God, I will not let it happen to my daughter."

Kat wanted to tell him that it wasn't that simple: he couldn't protect his daughter from something like this. But she also wasn't a parent, and Emma wasn't her daughter. So she just nodded, her throat tight, and was thankful that the nurse returned right then with Emma's backpack.

"I've let the front desk know that Emma's leaving early, and Mrs. Gentry knows as well." She handed the bag to Gavin. "Feel better soon, Emma."

Emma stood up and Gavin followed her out. He didn't say anything to the nurse or Kat as they left. Now he'd probably never speak to her again. She couldn't regret what she'd done, though. If Gavin needed time to accept to what was happening with Emma, that was his problem, not hers. She just hoped his stubbornness didn't make things worse in the end.

"That poor child," the nurse murmured. "I've never met one like her. But it's not a surprise, given who her mother is."

Kat stilled. She shouldn't pry, but her curiosity got the better of her. "Her mother?"

"Oh, you wouldn't know, would you? Teagan, her mother, she was famous around this town when those two were younger. She was the pretty cheerleader, and he was the awkward bookworm. When they got together, everybody was surprised." The nurse chuckled. "I guess opposites attract, right? Then they moved to the East Coast, and we barely heard anything about them, until suddenly they're splitting up and apparently Teagan is in treatment."

The nurse began organizing things on the counter, as if she didn't even see Kat standing there anymore. "And now this whole thing with their daughter." The nurse clucked her tongue. "Well, I guess the apple doesn't fall far from the tree, as they say."

Kat's stomach twisted. "I guess not," she replied before returning to her classroom. Silas was just getting the kids lined up to return to Mrs. Gentry's room, and he told her he'd take them so she could have a moment alone.

"Same thing as last time?"

Kat looked up as Silas entered the computer lab. Glancing at the clock overhead, she had about five minutes before she would go get the next class for the afternoon. She sighed, her chin in her hand.

"Yeah, just like when I found her in the closet. That poor girl." She suddenly felt utterly exhausted and rather wished she could take a nap under her desk for the next period.

"What are they doing for her? She can't keep coming to school and having these episodes." Silas frowned. "Did her dad say anything?"

She definitely didn't want to get into that particular subject, so she just shrugged. "Who knows? I just hope they can get her feeling better."

Silas was silent for a moment as he watched her. Then, in a quiet voice, he said, "You don't have to take this on too, you know."

"What do you mean?"

"Just that I know you often feel like you have to take care of people. But I don't think this is something you can fix. Not this time."

She stared at him. She felt exposed, like Silas had scooped out her innards and now she was left with a gaping hole. "I'm just trying to help."

He came around the desk, looking like he was about to reach out and touch her hand before thinking better of it. "Can I say something? As a friend?"

"Haven't you already said something?"

He laughed a little. "True. But I think we've gotten to know each other enough to be honest. I saw how you put your life on hold for your grandmother. You told me how you took care of your mother. I just wonder if sometimes you feel like you aren't complete unless you're caring for someone else."

Kat brushed an imaginary piece of dust from the desk. "What else was I supposed to do? Leave my family to rot? That hardly seems fair."

"You know that's not what I mean." This time, Silas did touch her hand. "Just that you're so used to being a caretaker that if you're not doing that, you're adrift. And I just wonder if you're in over your head with this situation."

Her head hurt. Her heart hurt. She understood what Silas

was saying, but at the same time, she wanted to tell him to keep his opinions to himself. Why did Silas feel the need to warn her away from Gavin, like she had no idea what she was getting into? Like he'd ruin her life given half a chance?

"I disagree with what you're saying, but thanks. I'll try not to do anything." She knew she was being flippant, but she didn't care. "I need to go get my class now."

He didn't argue, just stood aside so she could go to the door. She still felt his gaze on her back, like he wanted to say something else. The cynical part of her wondered if this was just Silas's attempt to get her to date him instead of Gavin, and then she felt instantly guilty for the thought. God, she needed a drink. Maybe several.

When she finally got home that night, she opened a bottle of wine and tried to empty her mind of everything. But when she checked her email, she saw dozens of emails telling her how much of a bitch she was, how she could fucking choke, and suddenly the stress of the day pushed too hard and she started crying. She stood in her grandmother's kitchen, wine-glass in one hand and her phone in the other, and she sobbed like her heart was broken.

I'm so stupid, she kept thinking. *I'm so very, very stupid.*

The sobbing petered off, and afterward, she felt rather silly and dramatic. She wasn't the one with a kid having episodes at school. She wasn't the one with an ex-wife who was ill. But that didn't help alleviate her heavy heart, which she carried with her as she tried to get some sleep that night.

CHAPTER EIGHT

The day after Emma's incident—what did they call it this time? the computer lab incident?—Gavin told himself he had every right to be angry at Kat and it was none of her business what he did in regards to his daughter. She didn't know Emma's history. How could he explain that the three times he had taken Emma to therapy, his daughter would become so panicked afterward that it was like talking a person off of a mental ledge? Every time had been worse than the time before. After the third therapist, Gavin had vowed never to put Emma through that ever again.

He told himself that as he got Emma to go to sleep the night after this incident. He told himself the same thing a day later, even though guilt had started to niggle at him. The day after that, he told himself he'd maybe been a little harsh, but he'd still been well within his rights to tell her to back off. He couldn't think about the look on her face, or how he'd probably screwed up everything with her already, and as he did work around the vineyard, he told himself Emma was all he should be thinking about anyway.

"So what did those grapes do to you?"

Gavin looked up from the vine he was harvesting to see Adam standing over him, hands on his hips. River's Bend was beginning its yearly harvest, and unlike the previous three years, this year looked to be a good one. Unless Gavin destroyed all the grapes he picked.

"Sorry," he muttered, plucking the next deep purple grape more gently. "Have a lot on my mind."

The rest of the workers were some distance away, as Gavin had arrived a little later. He was fine with being alone, anyway. The last thing he wanted to do was chat.

Except Adam didn't seem inclined to let him be alone. "How's Emma doing?"

"As good as you'd imagine, I guess."

Adam sighed. "Gavin, this is the second time this has happened. This isn't normal behavior."

No shit, Sherlock. Gavin ground his teeth in frustration. Since when did every non-parent want to give him parenting advice?

"I'm not taking her to see a therapist," he said as he moved down the vine. "You don't know..." He trailed off, swallowing past the dry lump in his throat. "You didn't see her afterward. I'm not doing that to her again."

"But you can't not do anything."

"Who's saying I'm doing nothing?" Gavin ripped off a grape that burst in his hand. He swore. "I'd appreciate it if you kept your nose out of my business."

That shut Adam up. Gavin felt bad for a second, but he refused to apologize. Since when had Adam cared about him or Emma? He hadn't exactly been around when Teagan had been falling apart. He'd been too wrapped up in this vineyard and his fiancée.

Now you're just being petty, his mind told him. He knew it, but at the moment, he wasn't inclined to shrug it off.

"I'm just trying to help. We're all just trying to help," Adam said quietly. "You can't keep pushing everyone away."

Gavin stood up, grabbing his basket. "I have work to do." He stalked off to join the rest of the harvesters, ignoring Adam's expression.

The day Teagan had tried to kill herself, Gavin hadn't wanted to call his family. But Julia Danvers had called anyway, and after that, Gavin had waited for Adam's call. For some reason, he had needed to hear from his older brother, who'd experienced his own tragedy when he'd lost his wife Carolyn in a car accident years previously. Adam had always had the answers when they'd been young. But after days of waiting, Adam had never called.

The anger and the resentment built in his chest now until he wanted to scream with it.

You can't keep pushing people away.

How was he pushing people away when those people refused to be there when he needed them? That was the real question.

Gavin worked the rest of the day in a haze, trying to forget everyone and everything. He didn't want to consider that he'd made his own mistakes, that maybe he hadn't recognized when others were reaching out to help but he'd rejected them.

By the evening, though, Gavin felt exhaustion swamp his limbs. Emma was similarly tired and silent, and the quiet apartment was almost painful. And of course, as he looked at the books Kat had gone through just days prior, his heart stuttered. God, he'd made a real hash of this, hadn't he? Kat didn't know what had happened with Emma in regards to therapists; she'd just been trying to help in the way she thought best. The guilt almost choked him. After Emma went to her room, he called Kat, but there was no answer. He left a voicemail, asking her to call him back.

The evening waned on, but no return call. He didn't want to press her, but when she didn't return his text, that guilt turned straight to worry. What if those threats she'd been receiving had manifested in something really dangerous? Now he couldn't stop thinking about all the horrible things that could've happened to her. He called her one last time, hoping she'd pick up and ream into him for being annoying, but nothing. Just voicemail. He left the apartment and knocked on Joy's door down the hallway.

"Gavin," she said with surprise, her bright purple hair piled on top of her head. "What is it?"

"I need to go see someone real quick. Can you stay with Emma until I get back?"

"What is it?" Adam stepped up behind Joy, putting his hands on her shoulders. "Gavin?"

Gavin stiffened at the sight of his brother, but he didn't have time for this. "I'll be right back. Will you watch Emma?"

"Of course. Do you need help?" Adam asked, concern lacing his voice.

"No, but thanks." Gavin had already grabbed his car keys, and he jogged down the stairs and out to his car before his brother decided to press for more information. His heart was pounding so fast he could barely keep his thoughts straight. Gripping the steering wheel, he drove as fast as he could to

Kat's place, praying with everything he had that he was just overreacting.

When he knocked on the door, no one answered. A chill swept through him. Going to the window, he knocked. "Kat! Are you in there?" The logical part of him wondered if she just wasn't home, but when he glanced into the garage, he saw her car. He tried the front door, but it was locked. "Kat! Open up! It's Gavin."

He heard a sound around back. Sprinting toward the sound, he first saw the bright red blood smeared across the ground before he saw Kat.

Oh God, she's been hurt. I'm too late.

She had her hands over her mouth as she stared at the scene on the ground. As Gavin got closer, he saw that the blood wasn't coming from her—thank God—but that someone had left a decapitated squirrel in the yard, a trail of blood covering the autumn leaves.

"Kat, Jesus Christ, what happened?" He took her hands away from her face, and he watched as she trembled, her face pale. She wasn't crying, which made him worry even more. "Are you all right?"

She nodded jerkily. "I'm okay. I mean, it's just a squirrel. Better a squirrel than me, right?" She laughed, and Gavin took that as a sign that he should embrace her. When she hiccupped against his shoulder, he knew he'd made the right decision.

He rubbed her back through her thin jacket. "Come on, let's go inside." He wanted to think the squirrel was just some leftover dinner from some predator, but he knew enough to tell that the squirrel had been killed with an ax of some sort by a human, not another animal. And if a person had done this, then they'd obviously left it here for a reason.

Kat pulled away, but only to rifle in her jacket to pull out a note. She handed it to Gavin. "This was left with it."

He unfolded the note to read: *You'll be next.* Fury swept through him. "What the fuck? God, Kat, we have to call the police."

"I know. I was just so freaked out I hadn't yet." She rubbed her arms, and Gavin led her inside, away from the bloody mess. "Who the fuck would do something like this?"

"Someone crazy, that's who." He took her into the living room and wrapped her in a blanket before pulling out his phone to call the police. "They'll be here in a few minutes," he said. He sat down next to her and placed an arm around her shoulders. She leaned against him and sighed. "Why the squirrel, though?"

She laughed, but it was bitter. "The game has a flying squirrel in it." She sniffled. "They knew exactly what they were doing."

"And all this over a game? What the hell is the game even about?"

She stiffened a little against him. "Nothing that horrible," she muttered.

Now she had his curiosity piqued. But when she didn't elaborate, he shook her slightly. "Come on, tell me. It can't be that bad."

"It's not bad. It was just a silly, satirical game. I was making fun of meninists." At his blank look, she laughed. "They're feminists, except the dude version. They're all about men's rights."

Gavin made a face. "And they're mad you were poking fun?"

"Basically."

He didn't really understand exactly what she was talking about, but he knew well enough that this was an extreme overreaction for something like an online game. He was about to tell her that it didn't matter what the game was about, that these threats weren't remotely okay, when someone knocked on the door.

The next two hours were spent with the police. They interviewed both Kat and Gavin, took photos of the poor headless squirrel, and then poured over all the comments and emails Kat had received as well.

Officer Haldon, who Gavin knew was involved with Jaime's case, took everything in in his usual, serious way, although he treated Kat gently, for which Gavin was grateful. She wasn't made of glass, but he didn't want things to be made worse for her, either, by overly probing questions or judgmental asides. Officer Haldon took notes and photos, asking pertinent questions before taking his leave, saying that if he found out anything or discovered any possible suspects, he'd be in touch shortly.

Gavin closed the door quietly, turning back to Kat, who looked so small wrapped up in the blanket he'd placed around her shoulders. Her face was drawn and tired, and at the thought of saying goodbye and leaving her here alone, he balked. What if something else happened? Whoever this was, he or she wasn't going to stop anytime soon.

"Stay with me tonight," he said before he even realized he'd been considering it.

She glanced up at him. "At your place?"

"Yeah. It'll be kind of cramped, but you can't stay here alone. I'd stay here with you, but with Emma and everything…"

She nodded, but she still looked dazed.

He sat down next to her and before she could protest, he hugged her close. The tension in her body loosened, and she relaxed against him, clutching at his shirt in small fistfuls.

Now that the police were gone and they could both finally breathe, Gavin gave in to the fear that had been eating at him. He hugged her so hard her breath stuttered, but he just needed her close. "When you didn't pick up your phone…" he muttered against her neck. "I was terrified, Kat. I thought something had happened to you. Even worse than some fucking squirrel."

She laughed, but the laugh turned into a little sob. She wiped her eyes underneath her glasses.

"Also, I wanted to tell you how sorry I am," he said. "I shouldn't have said what I did after what happened with Emma."

She just sighed. "I know you had your reasons, but I hope you know I meant well. I hate seeing Emma like that. I hate seeing *you* like that." She pulled away so she could look him in the eye. "You can't keep going like this, you know."

"Adam said the same thing." He hesitated, but he was too tired to keep everything in anymore. Stroking her arm, he murmured, "I took Emma to see a therapist. Three, actually. After what happened with her mother. Everyone told me it was the right thing to do."

Kat watched him with those deep brown eyes, and for some reason, he felt like he could tell her anything. He could bare his soul to her and she'd understand.

"But with each visit, she got worse. By the third one, she was hiding underneath our stairwell like a cornered animal. I just couldn't keep doing that to her." He ran his fingers through his hair. "How do I take her to a fourth person without something worse happening? How can I justify that to her?"

His voice was anguished, and Kat reached out to soothe him. "You were doing the best you could," she said. "I would've done the same. I think anyone would have."

"Would they? I don't know. Sometimes I feel like no matter what I do, things only get worse. I tried to save Teagan, but I couldn't. Now I'm terrified that I'm losing my daughter as well."

His throat closed and all he could do was try to calm his breathing, keep the memories at bay for now. He couldn't tell Kat about Teagan—it was still too raw—but she didn't press him. She just wrapped her arms around him, hugging him like he'd been hugging her earlier.

"I don't know what to do anymore," he admitted. "How do I fix something I can't understand in the first place?"

She didn't say anything for a moment. "I think you just have to keep trying. I'm not going to say you should go to another therapist, but maybe you could find someone else. Explain to them what's happening, and maybe at some point, they can meet Emma." She sighed. "I don't know, Gavin. But I do know that things can't get better without something changing."

He knew she was right, but it didn't help the heaviness in his heart. And then he realized that once again, he'd dumped his problems into Kat's lap. He'd come here to help *her*, but inevitably, she'd ended up helping him.

But this time, she wasn't going to be alone. He was going to take care of her and protect her from whatever this was. He wasn't going to let her get hurt. Too many people around him had gotten hurt in the last few years; Kat Williamson wasn't going to be added to that tally.

"Come on, get your things so we can get back to my place. I left Emma with Joy, but it's getting late." When she was silent, he asked, "If you're okay with this, of course. I can ask Joy to stay with Emma and I can stay here with you—"

She shook her as she stood up. "I don't want to stay here anyway. The thought of that squirrel in the backyard…" She shuddered. "I'm afraid its head will end up on my pillow."

She laughed, but Gavin couldn't. "That's not funny."

"I know, but I had to try. Just give me a few minutes." Before she went to her room, though, she leaned up and kissed him on the cheek like she had days prior. But this time, Gavin couldn't help but turn his face so their lips met. He growled as they kissed, and she let out a breathy sigh. He kissed her and told her without words that she meant something to him, that she was worth taking care of. That he'd keep her safe no matter what.

"Go get packed," he finally said in a low voice.

She nodded, looking dazed again.

He didn't know how he'd manage to keep his hands off of her with her staying at his place. He told himself he could do it if he tried, but who was he fooling? The thought of her sleeping in his bed—he'd sleep on the couch, of course— padding around his apartment like a lover would do? Seeing her come out of the bathroom after she'd showered, all wet and warm and glistening? He had to stifle a groan at the thought, and then he chastised himself for thinking dirty thoughts in a situation like this.

She isn't coming over so you can get laid, he told himself sternly.

After explaining to Joy and Adam what had happened as briefly as he could, Gavin showed Kat to his room. "I just washed the sheets, so you're in luck there."

"Well, thank you, all the same." She flashed him a small smile. "Are you sure, though? I can sleep on the couch just fine."

"No way," he growled. "You'll sleep in my bed, Kat."

Her eyes widened at his words, and he cursed himself. Had he really said that? He turned away, thinking he should probably give her space. "There are clean towels in the bathroom. Let me know if you need anything."

"Okay."

As Gavin lay on the couch later that night, he knew he wasn't going to get any sleep. He couldn't stop thinking about Kat in his bed, about Kat curled up underneath his comforter, her scent mixing with his own. He groaned and punched the pillow under his head.

He must have dozed off, though, because the next thing he knew, he heard a door open, and then as if in a dream, Kat was walking toward him. He sat up with a start.

"Everything okay?" he asked.

She nodded; he could just make her out in the dim light of the living room. "Just couldn't sleep. You too?"

He nodded.

She sat down next to him, and it took everything in him not to haul her into his lap and kiss her. This was going to be a very long night, he thought with an inner sigh.

CHAPTER NINE

As Kat lay in Gavin's bed, staring up at the ceiling, she knew she wasn't going to sleep tonight. For one, the sheets smelled like him, and she couldn't help but inhale that scent and think of kissing him. Thoughts of kissing only made her more awake than ever, and so by one in the morning, she'd given up all hope of sleeping.

She debated whether or not she wanted to make herself a cup of tea. Would she wake up Gavin if she did? But something warm sounded too good to pass up, and besides, she'd gotten good at being quiet when Lillian had been alive. Kat had gotten up so many times in the middle of the night for one reason or another as her grandmother had declined, losing more and more of herself to the dementia taking hold of her mind.

Kat sighed. Getting up out of bed, she snagged her robe and her glasses. She tiptoed past Emma's room and entered the living room to get to the small apartment kitchen. But when she saw a figure sitting up on the couch, she stifled a gasp. *Gavin.* It was just Gavin.

They stared at each other in the dark, although she could only make out the outline of him. After they'd ascertained that the both of them couldn't sleep, she sat down next to him. He flipped on a dim lamp next to the couch, which suddenly made their surroundings almost too intimate. Gavin was rumpled, his hair sticking up, and Kat had to restrain herself from touching those silken strands. His beard had grown so much lately, though, that she almost expected him to carry around an ax like some kind of rogue lumberjack.

Kat wiped her hands against her pajama bottoms. This had been a bad idea. If she thought she couldn't sleep in between Gavin's sheets? There was no way she'd get sleepy sitting next to him like this. She could practically feel the heat of his body seeping into her own.

"I was going to make some tea," she said as she hopped up again. "You want some?"

She didn't wait for his answer. She needed a second to recalibrate, to figure out what the hell she was doing. That very stupid part of her wanted to kiss him and, hell, touch him and take whatever this was to a new level. The more prudent part of her told her that Gavin Danvers wasn't remotely ready for a new relationship and Kat would just get hurt. But that prudent voice kept getting smaller and smaller, until she knew it'd vanish in a puff of smoke—especially if he touched her.

Finding the kettle, she almost dropped the stupid thing when she realized how badly she was shaking. Was it fear? Or desire? Probably both. She filled it with water and set it on the stove, staring at it without really seeing it as she weighed the pros and cons of this situation like the programmer she was.

Pro: Gavin was a great kisser, and he'd probably be a great lover.

Con: He'd just gotten divorced and seemed hung up on that still.

Pro: She'd get to have sex! She missed sex. It'd been too long.

Con: What happened after they had sex? They became friends with benefits? Or had a real relationship?

The kettle just started to whistle before Kat took it off, not wanting to make any more noise. She realized with an eye roll that she didn't even know if Gavin *had* tea. Luckily, she found a box of chamomile in the back of a cabinet. She pilfered some for herself and for him.

All these pros and cons meant nothing, she knew, if Gavin didn't want her. He'd kissed her—twice—but that didn't mean he wanted more than that. In her experience with men, that wasn't usually the case, but Gavin wasn't the usual kind of man.

"Tea?" She handed him a mug as she sat down on the couch, making sure they weren't close enough to touch.

He seemed nonplussed by the appearance of tea, and if the situation weren't so strange, Kat would laugh.

"Thanks," he replied gruffly. He sipped the brew before setting it on the coffee table in front of them. They sat in silence for a time until he asked, "Are you okay?"

She swallowed the hot tea. What a question! She'd been threatened multiple times over the past month, had kissed a man who seemed completely emotionally unavailable, and now she was in his apartment, wondering if sleeping with him was in her best interests.

She gripped her mug tighter. "I'm fine," she said, because

any other answer wasn't something she could get out right now.

"If you're scared about the threats, I'll keep you safe," he insisted. "I don't want you to be afraid."

Oddly enough, she wasn't. Or rather, she was, but it was with the knowledge that she wasn't alone in this. Gavin's presence and assurances meant more to her than she'd even realized. Her heart warmed as much as the tea warmed her body as she sat there next to him.

"Thank you. I mean, you've gone out of your way to help me. I don't know a lot of people who would do that."

He made a face, like he was uncomfortable. "I owe you. For helping Emma, for helping me. I care about you, Kat."

The words hung in the room. She swallowed against a suddenly dry throat. "I care about you, too," she murmured.

He shifted, moving closer toward her. She expected him to reach out and touch her, but he didn't. "Sometimes I'm not convinced you're real."

"Me? What do you mean?"

"Just that, even after everything that's happened, you're still so *together*. I would've expected any person to have kind of lost it by now."

Kat shrugged. "I'm not the type of person to weep and moan, if that's what you mean. What good will it do? You just have to keep moving forward. I've known that since I was a kid."

She knew it all too well, that breaking down wasn't something she had the means to do. She had to pick up the pieces, keep going. Brush the tears off of her cheeks and continue on.

He sighed. "I get that. There were days the past few years..." He stared at the steaming mug that he'd set on the coffee table, as if he could divine the secrets of humanity from its depths. "Some days Teagan would be so sick that I didn't know if she'd come out of it."

Kat saw how his shoulders were hunched, how he grimaced from the memories. "My mom died of breast cancer when I was fifteen," she said quietly. She hadn't planned on telling him that, but the words just spilled out. "It was just her and me for most of my life. My dad left when I was just a baby. We moved around a lot, but we were each other's constant. But when she got sick, I had to be the parent. I don't know how I managed to graduate from high school in the end, I missed so many days."

"I'm sorry, Kat."

She brushed away the tears that had sprung to her eyes. When had she become such a watering pot? "Thank you. She died a year after her diagnosis, and I went to live with my aunt and uncle. But I was determined to get out of there, so I graduated high school early and never looked back."

The pain of losing her mom had only lessened slightly in the subsequent years. Some days it was a faint ache, while other days it was acute. Tonight, Kat wished her mom were here to hug her, to tell her everything would be okay. *We'll be okay, babe,* she'd say. *Because you and me can do anything together.*

"Teagan wasn't always sick," Gavin said. "When we first dated, she was the girl who everyone wanted. Or wanted to be."

Kat couldn't help but smile. "And you had no idea why she'd date you?"

"Exactly. We married after college, but after Emma was born, things changed." He took in a deep breath. "She'd have these days where she wouldn't sleep—for days and days—and she'd be so happy and excited and she'd redecorate the entire house or something like that. But then she'd crash and burn, and become so depressed that she wouldn't get out of bed. By the time Emma was a toddler, I was the only one taking care of her." His hands balled into fists, "It got to the point that I was scared to leave Emma alone with her. Not because she'd hurt her, but because she might hurt herself."

"Was she ever diagnosed?"

"With bipolar. She went on medication, was good for a while, but she was never good about taking the medication. She'd relapse and it was a cycle. I tried to get her take her meds, get her to therapy, all of it. We'd get into these fights, and sometimes I got so angry that I had to leave the house."

He looked so alone that Kat set her mug down on the table and looped an arm under his. "Sounds like we've both had our fair share of shit."

He laughed a little. "To say the least." He inhaled and turned his gaze toward her. "I didn't mean to unload on you."

"And I didn't mean to unload on you, but here we are." The words drifted off into the space between them, and Kat couldn't look away from his penetrating gaze. His dark eyes caused her to shiver. He reached up and touched her cheek with a gentle caress.

"Do you wear this every night?" He touched the silk scarf she'd wrapped around her hair.

She'd forgotten she was wearing it. Suddenly self-conscious, she explained, "It protects my hair. Otherwise it'll break off and be a mess."

"Mmm, I do love your hair. Do you do it yourself?"

"For the most part. Sometimes I have help. It's hard to braid your own hair."

In a deadpan voice, he replied, "Considering I can barely braid Emma's, I understand completely."

She patted him on the chest. "It's okay. It takes practice. Although sometimes when I see Emma's hair, I have to restrain myself from redoing it."

"You're too kind," he said with a snort. "It's one of those things I'm working on. Because God knows Emma doesn't have anyone else around who's going to braid her hair."

Kat's heart clenched. She recognized that well of loneliness within him that she'd known for so many years. It was a strange thing, she knew, to bond over. But that kinship only intensified her attraction to him, and without thinking about it, she touched his shaggy hair, smoothed a finger across his eyebrows.

"Kat." His voice was barely more than a growl.

"Do you want me to stop?"

He didn't even hesitate. "Hell no. I just wanted to make sure you didn't want to."

She didn't know who kissed who, but their mouths met and it was like all the heat of the room exploded between them. Gavin snaked an arm around her waist while she pressed her hands against his hard chest, and the kiss deepened. His tongue met hers, and her entire body unfurled like a flower toward the sun. Yes, this was what she wanted. She didn't care what happened afterward. She just wanted him.

His heart beat wildly beneath her palms as she traced the lines of his collarbone, his sternum. He made a sound in the back of his throat. His beard scratched at her lips, but she found that she rather enjoyed that feeling. She'd usually kissed clean-shaven men, but everything about Gavin contradicted what she thought she'd preferred.

"How do you taste so sweet?" he muttered before kissing her cheek.

"It's probably the tea."

He shook his head. "It's that, but not. It's something else. I think it's just you." His mouth moved toward her jaw, and she leaned back slightly to give him access. "You've driven me insane since the first time I met you."

She sighed. "That time outside your apartment?"

He pulled away, but only so he could look into her eyes. "You looked so gorgeous; it drove me insane."

"Really? I just thought you didn't want to talk to me."

"I didn't want to talk to you."

She raised an eyebrow. "Is that supposed to be a compliment?"

"Let me rephrase that." He rubbed the back of his neck. "I wanted to talk to you, but I knew I'd bungle it, so I couldn't. I knew I could never have you."

She didn't want to point out that he was talking to her *now*, and saying more than he ever had before. She kissed him on the forehead, on his cheeks, light butterfly kisses that caused him to fist his hands in her robe against her back. When she reached his lips, her heart thrilled when he captured her mouth.

Things only progressed from there. She touched his shoulders while he trailed a hand under her robe and her shirt, reaching the bare skin of her lower back. Her ears buzzed and her heart pounded, and she transformed into a being of pure sensation. Suddenly feeling like she was wearing too many layers, she untied her robe and tossed it aside, now clad in only her thin shirt. Her nipples beaded against the material, and she saw the gleam in his eyes as he realized she wasn't wearing a bra.

Her breasts felt heavy, achy, and when he cupped one in his big palm, she let out a moan.

"Yes, touch me," she breathed into the night. "Please."

His thumb circled her nipple. She leaned backward until she was half-lying on the couch with him over her. He played with her other breast, but it wasn't enough. She arched against him, and he took the cue, trailing his hand up under her shirt to clasp her bare breast. Biting the inside of her cheek, she stifled a groan at the sensation of his fingers on her breast.

"Let me see you," he groaned. He tugged at her shirt hem with his other hand.

She wasn't going to stop him. Instead, she reached down and flung off the offending garment, now her breasts bare in front of him. He drank her in for a moment, and she couldn't help but preen a little under his admiring gaze.

"Damn, you're gorgeous." He smoothed a finger across a nipple, and she gasped at the sensation.

His hands played with her breasts, making her moan and breathe his name, and soon he replaced his hands with his mouth, sucking and nipping. He made her ache, made her wet and desperate. She'd never wanted a man as much as she wanted Gavin in this moment. It was a heady, all-consuming emotion, like a bottle of champagne. She was all bubbles and light.

He moved upward to kiss her mouth again. Reaching underneath his shirt, she felt the play of muscle and skin. She smoothed a fingertip around a mole she found, and when she traced a figure eight in the dip of his lower back, he shuddered, pressing his hardness against her. She shimmied and arched, wanting more friction, and in response, he kissed her harder.

Was she going to get off just from rubbing through their clothes? She hadn't been this turned on since she was a teenager. Licking at his mouth, she dipped her hand in the waistband of his sweatpants, which earned her a curse.

The kiss turned almost frantic then. Kat heard Gavin say her name, and then he was moving downward, kissing a trail down her torso. He hooked his hands in her pajama pants and was about to pull them off when they heard the creak of a door.

They froze. She looked at Gavin, and he looked at her. They gasped for air and just as footsteps sounded toward them, Kat grabbed a blanket to cover herself and Gavin grabbed her shirt to stuff behind his back as Emma walked into the room.

The girl blinked at them, rather like a sleepy owl. She yawned. "I thought I heard a noise," she said.

Kat's face flamed, and she pulled the blanket closer around her shoulders. Gavin got up, giving her a brief glance, and promptly herded Emma back into her room. "Kat and I were just talking," Kat heard him say before shutting Emma's door.

Kat collapsed onto the couch. Her heart was still pounding frantically, and she couldn't get her body to calm down. If she were anywhere else, she'd take care of this problem herself, but then again, this had been a perfect wake-up call. Was she really going to sleep with Gavin and hope it didn't all go to hell afterward? She snorted. She wasn't *that* stupid.

Sighing, she got her shirt and pulled it over her head, and

then grabbed her discarded robe and made her way back to Gavin's room. She really didn't want to have some awkward *this shouldn't have happened* conversation with him.

But as luck would have it, Gavin came into the bedroom and shut the door, saying in a soft voice, "Are you still awake?"

She rolled her eyes in the darkness. "I'm not going to be sleeping anytime soon."

He seemed to hesitate. Kat rolled over, although she couldn't make out his face in the darkness.

"Look, Kat—"

She held up a hand. "Don't. I don't have the juice for whatever it is you're going to say. We're adults, and we did nothing wrong. It's just bad timing. It's fine, Gavin."

My heart will be perfectly, completely, utterly fine. Or so I'll tell myself.

He sighed. "Okay. Good night, then."

After he shut the door and padded back to the living room, Kat punched the pillow next to her. She didn't know if she was glad, mad, or sad: glad that it had happened, mad that it had ended, or sad that it couldn't happen again.

"Penny for your thoughts?"

Kat jumped, and Silas laughed at her expression. "Jesus, you scared me!" she said.

He handed her a cup of coffee. "Sorry. I know you're on edge lately, and for good reason." He looked her over. "How are you doing?"

Instead of answering, she sipped her coffee.

"I'm doing all right. I got the window boarded up at the

house, and they were able to clean off the paint." She sighed. At the moment, she was on her lunch break at school, and she'd rather hoped to keep to herself. But Silas was her friend, and she knew he was worried about her. He also knew about her predilection for coffee in the early afternoon, bless him.

"Are you still staying at Gavin's place?" He didn't look at her when he asked the question, which made Kat tense.

"For now, yeah. I'd rather not be alone if something else should happen."

Silas grimaced. "Just thinking about what could've happened to you." He turned toward her, his gaze serious. "You know you can always stay with me, right?"

"I do. Thank you." She pressed his hand. "Seriously. You've been a lifesaver these past few weeks."

"Kat..." His knee brushed hers, and then his hand was on her elbow. "Have you thought about what I asked? I mean, about us?" When she didn't reply, he added, "I know it's a bad time. I do. But I'm worried about you. I could help you. Take care of you. And I'm not sure Gavin Danvers is the best man to do it."

That caused her to bristle. She set her coffee down on the bench. "Do you even know Gavin?"

"I know enough about him. I know that he's messed up from his marriage, and that he's not going to commit to anyone. Not right now. And not with his daughter having issues." Silas's eyes were beseeching, and Kat couldn't find the strength to argue with him. "I care about you, Kat." He made a noise in the back of his throat. "That's not true—I mean, I love you. I love you, Kat."

Kat sat there, stunned. She'd known Silas was interested in her and cared about her, but *love*? It was too much, and with everything going on. She slumped next to him, so exhausted she couldn't even move away.

"Kat, say something."

"I can't, Silas." Her voice was a whisper, and he had to lean toward her to hear her. "Not right now. I'm sorry. I do care about you, though. As a friend." She grimaced at that, but it was true. He was a friend, and had always been just that.

Silas took his hand from her elbow. He stared off in front of them, and she wondered if he was angry. But when he spoke, it wasn't anger lacing his voice. It was resignation. "You're in love with him, aren't you?"

Her world tilted on its axis. She almost blurted out a denial, but she bit her tongue. "I don't know," she answered, her heart pounding in her chest.

"I think you do know, and I wish you weren't. Not just for me—although I'm selfish enough to admit that's part of it—but because I think you're going to get your heart broken." He rose from the bench, but not before adding, "Just, watch yourself, Kat. Don't do anything you'll regret."

Her emotions were so snarled that she couldn't figure out how she felt. Part of her was angry at Silas's warning, while another part of her was terrified he was right. Did she love Gavin? Maybe she did. Maybe she'd fallen for him the first time they'd kissed, or when she'd seen him taking care of Emma.

She took a deep breath and finished her coffee, almost laughing at everything that had been happening. Gavin Danvers had already gotten under her skin and, she was afraid deep inside her heart that she was only going to get hurt in the end.

CHAPTER TEN

Gavin realized the irony that was his life when he wanted the woman who was currently staying at his apartment and driving him crazy. Not because she was a bad houseguest. No, she was the ideal houseguest, he had to admit: clean, quiet, and she cooked. But it was seeing her walk around his apartment, seeing her toothbrush next to his on the bathroom counter, and smelling her scent everywhere that drove him insane. It was like having a wife again.

And he really, really didn't need to think of Kat as his wife.

It didn't take long for word to get around town about what had happened. Joy had stopped by Gavin's to see Kat, and Adam had also dropped in, asking if they could help in any way. Soon it seemed like everyone in town wanted to help: Grace, Jaime, even Gavin's parents, along with every person who had ever talked to Kat. Her coworkers from school stopped by in droves, bringing casseroles and other dishes, hugging Kat and offering her various condolences. And then, of course, there were the raised eyebrows about a single man offering Kat a place to stay. Heron's Landing was a small enough town where something like that raised eyebrows and created whispers, but Gavin refused to let that stop him. Let the old biddies gossip; he wasn't going to let Kat get hurt just because some people thought it was *unseemly* for her to stay at his apartment.

One of the people who stopped by more than once was Kat's friend and coworker, Silas Fraser. Gavin had only met the man a few times, and he'd seemed innocuous enough. But after he'd come into the living room to see Silas's hand on Kat's knee, Gavin had gritted his teeth so hard they'd practically turned to dust in his mouth. That green snake of jealousy had coiled in his gut, and he knew it was ridiculous of him. For one, Kat could date whomever she wanted—Gavin had no real claim on her. He hadn't exactly asked her out, anyway. And if she preferred Silas with his gap teeth, so be it.

But that didn't stop him from getting absurdly tense anytime the other man stopped by, bearing all sorts of gifts. Flowers, takeout, some books. Mostly it was the way he looked at Kat: like she were too beautiful to exist on planet earth. How Kat didn't see it, Gavin had no idea.

Working at River's Bend that afternoon, Gavin told himself he was being an idiot. He couldn't stop thinking about his encounter with Kat, though, and all he could see in his mind's eye was the way she'd looked, bare to the waist as he'd kissed her. How her breasts had been the perfect size for his palms, how the dark brown nipples had strained for his attention, and how she'd moaned and undulated underneath him...

He swore as he stood, currently finishing up helping with the harvest. It was a cool day, but Gavin was wearing a thin short-sleeved t-shirt, mostly because he'd felt overheated for days now. Maybe some manual labor would kick some sense into him, he thought morosely.

The worst part of it all was that he knew he couldn't have Kat. She deserved better than a man who was too broken, too emotionally fucked up, to give her the kind of relationship she wanted. They could get along fairly well for a while, he admitted, but inevitably, she would need more. She'd want commitment, family, the whole nine yards. And Gavin knew he couldn't give her those things. He'd done it once before, and it had fallen apart despite all his attempts to keep things together.

Given his foul mood, everyone at the vineyard gave him a wide berth. Even Adam didn't try to talk him out of his mood, for which he was perversely grateful. He wasn't particularly interested in his older brother telling him he was screwing up. Besides, Adam was too busy with Joy and their upcoming wedding to really understand what was going on with Gavin.

By midafternoon, Gavin was walking toward the barn with his basket of ripe grapes when he felt his phone vibrate in his hip pocket. After Emma's episodes, and now the threats against Kat, he'd made sure to carry his phone everywhere with him. His heart pounded each time he got a call, although more often than not, it was some spam call. He set down the basket and pulled out his phone, and when he saw it was Kat herself, fear congealed his blood.

"Kat, are you okay?" He probably shouldn't have assumed something was wrong, but dammit, he was worried about her —and for good reason, too.

He heard an intake of breath on the end of the line before she responded. "I'm okay...I mean, I'm not, but I am." She laughed, but it sounded more like a sob. "I stopped by the house today to get some things, and they've broken in a window and written something on the side of the house."

He stopped in his tracks. Now all he could feel was pure, crystallized anger. "They did *what*? I'll be right there. Have you called the police?"

"That was my next call. See you soon."

Gavin said goodbye, and after retrieving his things and telling Adam what had happened, he sped off to Kat's house, his heart in his throat. He knew Kat well enough now to know that her supposed calm was just a mask. She was so good at holding it all together, but she had to be terrified. How long could she last before breaking down?

By the time he arrived, the cops were there, flashing red lights surrounding the property. Kat stood off to the side, Officer Haldon once again questioning her. Gavin stepped out of the truck and headed toward her, but not before he was arrested by the sight of the words DIE WHORE written in red paint on the side of the house.

"Son of a bitch," he breathed. His vision awash in a red fury, he had to restrain himself from yelling in sheer rage. But when he turned to see Kat hugging herself, looking tired and small, he knew he couldn't give in to his anger. Not yet. She needed him.

"Kat, are you all right?"

Before she even replied, he hauled her into his arms. Officer Haldon paused with whatever he'd been saying and then murmured something about giving them a moment. Gavin didn't particularly care what the other man did; he just wanted to make sure Kat was okay. He ran his hands down her body, checking for injuries, even though he knew she didn't look injured. She said as much, but he had to know for sure.

"I'm okay, Gavin," she said. "I just got here, and whoever did this had already run off."

He looked into her face, and she was as dry-eyed as always. So calm, so put-together. But he saw the way a muscle twitched in her cheek, how big the dark circles had gotten underneath her eyes, how she was hunching in on herself. He rubbed her arms.

"I won't let anything happen to you," he vowed in a low voice. "I promise you that much. We'll find who did this."

She nodded and laid her head on his shoulder. He rubbed her back.

He wondered how long she'd stay together, how long she could be strong for herself and everyone else around her. *You're always the one taking care of everyone else*, he thought. *But who's taking care of you, darling Kat?*

Everything became a whirlwind of questions and photos and statements, but Gavin didn't leave Kat's side for a second. Officer Haldon told Kat that they hadn't found any leads, but this case was their top priority. After assuring Kat that they'd add a police presence to watch the house, he assured her that they would make certain she wouldn't be hurt.

"This person wants to keep you scared," Officer Haldon said, his voice disgusted. "But we won't let that happen. As much as we possibly can, ma'am."

Kat nodded tiredly. "Thank you for all your help."

"After you get that window boarded up, you can stay here if you'd like. The police will be watching twenty-four seven."

Gavin stiffened at the thought of her staying here alone. There was no way in hell he was going to let that happen. But

Kat spoke before he did. "I don't think I want to stay here tonight, but again, thank you." She held out her hand, and Officer Haldon shook it with a slight frown.

When Gavin and Kat arrived back at his place, it was just the two of them, as Emma wouldn't be home from school for another two hours.

"I only had to teach a half day today," Kat said by way of explanation, "and I wanted to check on the house. And then…" She sighed. "This person sure isn't giving up. I guess I have to give them props for consistency."

The attempt at a joke fell flat, and Gavin couldn't even try to laugh. He handed her a cup of tea. After that first night, he'd made sure to stock every flavor of tea he could buy at the local store, although Kat had assured him that plain old black tea was perfectly fine.

"Mike told me that this jasmine tea is good," he explained.

Her mouth quirked into a smile. "I'm not sure how much of a tea connoisseur Mike is, but I'll take his word for it."

She sipped her tea in silence. He didn't want to press her to talk. But as she drank her tea, he could see her hands starting to shake; eventually, she was shaking so hard that he took the mug from her, worried she'd spill the hot liquid on her fingers.

"I was so scared," she gasped. "When I saw what they'd written on the house, I was sure they were still there, just waiting to hurt me." She swallowed, and her eyes were wild when she looked at him. "They're going to kill me, aren't they?"

Gavin's heart lurched. He pulled her into his arms and held her tight, her words terrifying him. "Not without killing me first," he vowed.

She clutched at him, like she couldn't get close enough. He could feel her heart pounding wildly, like a bird fluttering against its cage doors.

"I was so scared, so scared, oh my God, *Gavin*." She kept saying the same thing over and over again, her entire body trembling, and he didn't know how to make her feel safe. He felt utterly useless, but at least he could hold her, keep her close, and murmur things in her ear. He could rub her back and tell her he'd never let anything happen to her.

She kept trembling, though, and soon he heard her breath hitch. That was when she started crying: in deep, rolling sobs, she was crying so hard that he was afraid she'd hyperventilate. He let her cry until his shirt was soaked with her tears, but he didn't care. He knew someone like Kat didn't let her guard down easily. He doubted she'd cried even once since all this had started. So all the fear and anger and grief came out in one intense burst of tears that finally petered out after what seemed like an eternity.

She took off her glasses to wipe her eyes, her cheeks tear-streaked. She looked exhausted and yet, inexplicably, absolutely beautiful. He kissed her on the lips, but it was a tender kiss. It didn't suggest anything other than affection and reassurance. Afterward, he tucked her head underneath his chin and held her until she dozed off in his arms.

He carried her to his bed, stripping off her boots before placing a blanket on top of her. He changed his wet shirt, and soon after, Emma arrived home from school.

"Kat's taking a nap," he said, "so let's be quiet, okay?"

Emma nodded, frowning. "Why is she taking a nap? Is she sick?"

"Kind of. She had a hard day." Gavin wasn't going to tell

Emma what had happened. It would just terrify her, and he didn't need both Kat and Emma crying. "Did you have a good day at school?"

Emma pulled her pant leg up to show him her knee. "I fell off the tire swing and got this. But I didn't even cry."

It was a rather impressive bruise, he had to admit. "How did you fall off the tire swing, anyway?"

"We were standing on it and then Danny made it go so fast that I fell off. I had to lie still underneath it until it stopped turning, otherwise it would've hit me in the head."

Honestly, sometimes he wondered how any child survived elementary school. "And are you supposed to be standing on the tire swing?"

She shrugged. "No, but Ms. Reeves has a crush on Mr. Loy and doesn't pay much attention while on recess duty if he's around."

Emma recounted the rest of her day, which included various bits of teacher-related gossip that both amused and rather astonished Gavin—mostly due to the fact that Emma knew of such gossip in the first place—while Kat slept the afternoon away. He heard her get up around five o'clock, but she didn't come out into the living room. He couldn't blame her. He was the type of person who needed space after something so emotional, and he imagined Kat was similar. But that didn't stop him from knocking on the door and asking if she needed anything, to which she'd replied that she was fine.

"I heard someone broke into Ms. Williamson's house," Emma said as he started making dinner that evening.

He stilled. "Who told you that?"

Another shrug. "I heard it on the bus. So it's true? Is that why she's staying with us?"

"Yes, but I don't want you talking about it in front of her. It'll upset her."

"What if the burglar comes here, though?"

He recognized that tone in Emma's voice, which could so easily blossom into full-blown anxiety. Turning to look her in the eye, he said, "That won't happen. I promise. You know I'll keep you safe, right?"

Emma didn't look totally convinced, but he made sure to distract her with helping with dinner to make her forget her fear. It worked—at least for now.

CHAPTER ELEVEN

When Kat woke up, it was already dark out. She fumbled for her phone and groaned at the time displayed: nine o'clock. Now she'd never sleep. She stared up at the ceiling, dimly registering that she'd somehow ended up in Gavin's bed, and not for the reasons she would've preferred.

Sighing, she rose and went into the living room, where she found Gavin reading. He looked up when she entered.

"How are you feeling?" He got up to lead her to the couch.

"Tired, but I'll be okay." Embarrassment made her edgy. She hadn't cried like that in front of someone since her mom had died. Kat wished she could bury herself underneath a rock and maybe hide there for the foreseeable future. When she glanced at Gavin, she saw that his expression was full of concern, and she had to admit, it made her even antsier.

"I think I'll go home tomorrow," she said out of the blue. She hadn't even thought about it, but she needed distance. Time. Space to think about what the hell she was doing.

Having sex with a man was one thing; crying like a baby against his shoulder was another.

His dark eyebrows winged upward. "Are you sure that's a good idea?"

No, but it's better than being here, with you. "The police are watching the house, and I'd hate to intrude further."

"Don't even worry about that. I don't want you staying somewhere where you aren't safe." His eyes darkened, and now she couldn't look away. "I told you I'd keep you safe, and I meant it."

Kat didn't know if she wanted to turn tail and run, or launch herself into his embrace more. She hadn't had someone to look out for her for so long. Lillian had done her best after her mom's passing, but she'd been too far away to do much. And then she'd been diagnosed with dementia, and the grandmother Kat had known for twenty-five years had disappeared.

She hugged herself. "I think it's for the best if I go home," she said quietly.

"Is this about what happened last night?" His voice was little more than a growl, and it caused the hairs on the back of her neck to prickle.

"No, I mean, kind of..." She looked away from him. "It's more that I don't think we should continue what we're doing."

He didn't say anything to that. She knew, deep in her gut, that she was taking the easy way out. But she'd rather bring everything to a halt now before she got in so deep that she'd get her heart broken.

He rose from the couch and began pacing. He looked rather like a grumpy lion, all rumpled and glorious and scowling. Her heart—her stupid, stupid heart—fluttered as she watched him. Even now, she still wanted him.

"You can't leave," he said, and she blinked at him. "I mean, it's your choice, but it's a stupid one. You'll put yourself in danger, and for what? Because you regret what we did the other night?"

"I never said I regretted it."

"You're acting like you did."

She rolled her eyes. "Don't put words in my mouth, Gavin. I'm trying to be cautious. I'm trying not to screw myself over, okay?"

"And how, exactly, would you screw yourself over?"

She realized what she'd said, but she refused to apologize. "Look, I know you're not ready to move on from your divorce. I get it. It takes a while to get to that place, and I don't want to be your rebound chick."

He stared at her. Then he cursed. "You would not be my rebound chick."

"Maybe, maybe not. But I also don't want to be the other woman in your relationship."

"What the hell does that mean?"

"You know what it means!" She rose and pointed a finger at his chest. "How can we have a relationship if you're still not over your ex-wife? Or your marriage? You haven't exactly been interested in making this anything more than a fling, and I'm telling you, I don't want to have just a fling."

He gaped at her, but then he narrowed his eyes at her. "I assure you," he said in a low voice, "I'm over my marriage. I have been for years. It ended way before we ever filed for divorce." He took her hand that still had her finger pointed against his chest, and he lifted it to his mouth, kissing her fingers. She had to keep her knees from buckling, just from that simple caress. "That doesn't change the fact that I want you more than I've ever wanted another woman. And I think you feel the same way."

She couldn't deny it: she desired him, like she'd desire water in the middle of a desert. As he kissed her fingers, she didn't pull away. Instead, she found herself moving closer, until she was pressed against him, her breasts against his chest and his hardness against her belly.

She knew she should resist. She shouldn't give in. Another voice whispered that her accusations were just because she was scared, but didn't she have a reason to be scared? Letting herself trust and lean on another person—on this man—was a gamble she didn't know if she could take. And especially not on a man who'd experienced his own heartbreak that had left him bleeding and fractured.

All of that was pushed aside when he sucked her index finger into his mouth. The wet heat of his mouth stunned her, and she could feel herself growing painfully aroused. He let her finger go with a last lick of his tongue.

"We can't," she breathed. "Emma..." It was her last excuse.

"She's at Joy's for the night."

They stared at each other, knowing what that meant. There was no reason to say no. There was nothing to hold them back.

So Kat made a decision: she wasn't going to hold back anymore.

Wrapping her arms around his neck, she kissed him, and he groaned deep in his throat at the contact. His muscular arms hugged her close and almost stole the breath from her lungs. But she didn't care: she just wanted to get as close to him as possible.

They stood in the living room, kissing and licking and touching, and then Gavin reached down and lifted her up into his arms. She squeaked a little, and then squeaked again when he brought her down on his bed, still kissing her. His hands roved all over her body, like they couldn't stay in one place for too long, like he had to feel every inch of her skin. She felt the same. She reached underneath his shirt and skimmed her nails down his spine, which caused him to shudder in her arms.

"You have too much clothing on." She tugged on the hem of his shirt.

"So do you." He lifted her shirt off, and then she did the same for him. His eyes gleamed as he saw her in her bra, and feeling daring, she stripped out of her jeans, glad that she'd thought to wear something other than her cotton boy-shorts.

"Damn, Kat." His gaze drank her in. "You're gorgeous."

She stared at his chest, muscular and lightly dusted with dark hair, and she found her mouth watering. She sat up and began skimming her fingers across his chest, loving how warm and solid he was. She'd missed this, having a man so close, having him at her mercy. And the fact that it was Gavin Danvers? Made it even better.

She played for a few moments, but seeing his eyes narrow to tiny slits, she knew his self-control wasn't going to last. She unbuckled his belt and then palmed his erection through his jeans, which made him curse. Smiling, she traced his length, her heart pounding and her center becoming slicker.

Gavin, though, wasn't going to sit there and take what she doled out. He reached inside her silk panties, and she gasped when he parted her damp folds. He thrust a finger inside of her as his palm rubbed against her clit, and she let out a mewl when he barely brushed his hand against that aching bud. Her hand fell away from his cock without even realizing it.

She felt herself reaching toward climax, and when Gavin added a second finger, that was enough to send her off. He caught her moan of completion with a deep kiss. She shuddered and shook as they collapsed onto the bed together.

But Kat wasn't going to go down without a fight. She flipped him onto his back and climbed up onto his lap, undoing the buttons on his jeans and taking out his cock. God, his cock was amazing: long and hard, and she couldn't help but lick the tip before sucking it into her mouth.

"Fuck," he hissed as she licked him. "Goddamn, Kat, you're going to kill me."

She rather hoped she did. She smiled, taking more of his length into her mouth, but after a few more minutes, he pulled her up. "I want to come inside you," he said before reaching into the nightstand for a condom. He handed her the foil packet, which she managed to tear open and roll the latex down his cock despite her shaking hands.

She rose up over him, letting his cock brush against her. She was still wearing her panties, but that somehow made it more erotic, like they wanted each other so badly they couldn't take the time to fully undress. She rubbed against him, his cock glancing off of her still-sensitive clit, and they both hissed in a breath.

He palmed her ass. A flush had darkened his cheekbones, and his chest rose and fell in heavy breaths. As he watched her, she pulled the crotch of her panties aside and fitted his length against her sheath. And then she slowly sat back and impaled herself on him. It was pure ecstasy: full and hot inside of her, and she flexed herself around him just to hear him groan.

"God, Kat, you're going to kill me," he said again as he reached behind her and unhooked her bra, freeing her breasts to his hungry mouth as he sat up against the headboard. He sucked her nipples as she began to ride him, her hands on his shoulders as she used him as leverage.

"Gavin, Gavin, Gavin." She couldn't stop saying his name, couldn't stop moaning as she rode his cock, feeling him impale her over and over again, his hot mouth still playing with her breasts.

Another orgasm coiled in her belly, and she picked up her rhythm, which caused him to grab her ass and move with her. The combined effort sent her into a tailspin, and she was so close to catching that second climax that she could taste it on her tongue.

"I'm so close." She gripped his shoulders as she ground against him.

He reached between them, and he rubbed her clit with his thumb. She groaned to the ceiling. "Come for me," he breathed against her neck. "Come for me, my beautiful Kat."

That was all she needed. Her climax exploded over her, and she milked his cock with every spasm. He moaned as he started to come with her. Her vision filled with stars, and she had to grip his shoulders to keep herself from floating away entirely.

When she collapsed against him, both of them panting and sweaty, her mind felt strangely, blessedly empty. She breathed and kissed his neck, not wanting to part from him or even leave this bed. If she could, she'd stay here for the rest of her life.

But reality always came calling, and eventually, he nudged her off of him. She complied with a sigh, rolling onto the bed as he got rid of the condom. When she realized that her glasses had steamed up, she couldn't help but laugh.

"Do I want to know why you're laughing?" He lay down next to her and wrapped his arms around her.

"I was laughing because that was the most ridiculous sexual encounter I've ever had." She poked him in between his furrowed brows, and couldn't help but laugh again.

"If by ridiculous you mean fucking amazing, then I agree," he said as he grabbed her ass. "If I were ten years younger, I'd do it all over again."

She released a heavy sigh. "I guess I could endure it a second time..."

That earned her a smack on her ass, which made her squeak and then burst out laughing. He looked rather like a bear now, instead of a rumpled lion. Definitely a carnivore, she thought to herself, and quite liable to eat her up in one gulp if she weren't careful.

They cuddled for a while longer before Kat got up, mostly because she needed to take a shower. Gavin sighed as he let her rise, and then he sighed again when she made a point to bend down in front of him to pick up her discarded bra.

"Go take a shower, otherwise I'm hauling you back into this bed," he growled.

She winked at him over her shoulder. "Promises, promises."

After she took a quick shower, she went into the kitchen

to find Gavin stirring something. She sniffed the air, then wrinkled her nose. "Are you making ramen?"

"Yep." He flipped off the burner knob and doused the noodles and water with the sodium-packet flavor packets. "I made you some, too. Gourmet and all."

It was so stupid, but her heart fluttered at the gesture. The man was making her a heart attack in a bowl, and she was getting gooey feelings over it? She wanted to slap her own forehead. Hadn't she just told herself she wasn't going to do this? And look what had happened. She'd had the best sex of her life and was about to profess her undying love because Gavin had made her chicken-flavored ramen noodles.

She stilled at the word *love* floating through her mind. She refused to think she was in love with him. Infatuation? Yes. Desire? Absolutely. But love? She couldn't. She *wouldn't*.

But as he kissed her and made her laugh the rest of the evening, his hands roaming everywhere, she knew her arguments against the idea of loving Gavin Danvers were flimsy at best. And that was what scared her the most: that she'd given her heart to him without even putting up a fight in the first place.

CHAPTER TWELVE

"Dad, I can't wake up Mom. Please come home."

Gavin had been at work when Emma had called him after finding Teagan unconscious on the bathroom floor. As he'd left work, he'd called 911 and prayed to every deity he could think of that his wife wasn't already dead.

"I'll be there as fast as I can. Can you go to the front door and make sure to open it if the police get there before me?"

He didn't want to think about how calm his seven-year-old daughter was in the face of this trauma, or how he had to ask her to be there to let the paramedics in to help Teagan. He didn't think about anything as he drove home. Anger roiled through him with such intensity that at a stoplight, he had to lay his forehead on the steering wheel to catch his breath.

How could she do this? he couldn't stop thinking. It was the mantra running through his mind when he arrived home to see an ambulance with its lights flashing out front and a fire truck not far behind. It was the thought that wouldn't leave him when he found Emma in the living room, waiting for him. They were the words he couldn't shake as he watched the paramedics take Teagan out of the house on a stretcher after they'd told him she was alive but needed to have her stomach pumped.

Gavin didn't like to leave Teagan alone with Emma, but she'd been doing better lately, so he'd given in when she'd told him to stop hovering. He'd gone to work like it was any other day. But that had all ended when Teagan had decided she'd prefer to take a bottle of painkillers in her suicide attempt, leaving her own daughter to find her.

Gavin had kept those memories at bay recently, but Teagan had called him this morning to talk to Emma. Everything had come rushing back, and as he worked at River's Bend today, all he could see was Teagan's lifeless body on that stretcher, and the wide eyes of his daughter, who'd never been the same since.

He knew, logically, he shouldn't blame Teagan for what she'd done. She was ill. But anger still roiled in his gut anyway, and today it came back in a flood of resentment and fury. Not so much for himself, but for Emma. How could a mother do that to her own daughter?

He leaned against the wall behind the vineyard's main building, closing his eyes. He tried to get himself in check, but he could hear Teagan's voice teasing his senses. *I hope you guys are doing okay,* she'd said in that voice he'd gotten to know better than his own. *I miss you. Both of you. But I'm doing better now.*

He was glad she was doing better, but it was too late to feel anything but an exhausted kind of gratitude. Teagan was no longer his wife, and until she was really better, she wasn't a mother, either. She loved Emma—he knew that—but her absence still hurt them both.

The worst part of it was the feeling that he'd failed them. He couldn't save Teagan, and now, he wasn't sure he could save Emma, either.

"Gavin."

He looked up to see Kat walking toward him, and he blinked, wondering if he was seeing things. For some reason, seeing her here seemed out of place. Today she wore black jeans and a bright yellow top, her hair in her usual afro. He swallowed against a suddenly dry throat. Had it really been only half a day since he'd had her in his bed? He hardened instantly just from sheer proximity, and it took all his strength not to push her up against the wall behind him and take her again.

"What are you doing here?" he asked.

She shrugged. "I tried to find some kind of excuse, like you'd left something at the apartment, but there's no point in lying. I wanted to see you." She stepped closer, her hands in her pockets. "Stupid, right? It's not like I wasn't going to see you later this evening."

"Not stupid at all." His voice was hoarse, especially when she pressed her hands against his chest.

"Sometimes I wonder if this is all a dream," she murmured. "If I'll wake up and be alone again, if I've conjured you into being." She gazed up at him, her dark eyes wide. "You are real, right?"

He laughed a little. "As far as I know, yes."

It was inevitable that he'd kiss her. She stood on the balls of her feet as they kissed, and he wrapped his arms around her. She tasted like sweetness and light, her lips silky and soft. He pressed his hardened cock against her, just because he wanted her to know how he felt every time she was near.

"I want to take you until you forget your own name." He licked her jaw, and she shuddered. "Make you come until you scream."

"Then do it."

It was like something burst inside of him. With a groan, he moved so she was against the wall behind them, knowing that everyone had gone home for the day. But that didn't stop a thrill from running through him at the idea of getting caught. For Kat, it was worth it.

He scattered kisses across her cheeks and down her throat, tonguing the indentation between her collarbones. She ran her fingers through his hair and her hands moved up his shoulders as he feasted.

He kneeled in front of her, and she looked down at him with heat in her eyes. "Let me taste you," he muttered, unbuttoning her jeans to get to her wet center.

Her head thunked against the wall behind her when he pulled her panties down to her knees. "Gavin, are you sure? Outside?"

"Nobody's around." He kissed her hip, fluffing the curls hiding her core. "Let me do this."

She sighed. "Don't let me be the one to say no to having a guy go down on me."

He laughed. Parting her, he took in her musky scent, laving her with his tongue. She let out a moan that turned higher pitched when he licked her over and over. Her wetness coated his tongue, and God Almighty, he couldn't get enough. When he inserted the tip of his tongue inside of her, she shivered. He held her to his mouth, not letting her get away.

He played with her, building her climax, and when he only circled her clit, she swore at him. He smiled. Just as she was about to throttle him, he sucked her clit into his mouth and drew on it, the bud swollen and begging for his touch. She said his name over and over again as she clutched at his head. When he pushed a finger inside of her as he tongued her clit, she shimmied and shook, and he felt her sheath contract around his finger before her orgasm burst upon her.

She arched against him, but he didn't let her go until he'd milked every contraction from her. "Jesus Christ," she kept muttering, breathing hard. "Jesus motherfucking Christ."

He stood up and fumbled with his clothing, but not before pulling a condom from his wallet. Her lips quirked into a smile as she took it from him. "Somebody was prepared," she said.

"Thank God for that." He groaned when she rolled the latex down his cock, and then he groaned again when he pushed at her entrance. She took hold of his cock and then he was sheathed inside of her wet heat. "Fuck, you feel amazing."

"So do you." Her breath warmed his throat. "Take me, Gavin."

He didn't need to be told twice. He hooked his hand underneath her leg for leverage, pumping inside of her in a ruthless rhythm. Licking her throat, he felt his cock get even harder as he fucked her. She moaned and dug her nails into his shoulders, and the sound of their lovemaking only heightened his arousal.

When he felt her squeezing around his cock, he thrust harder, brushing against her clit with each movement. He saw her pupils dilate right before she reached climax, her nails digging even harder into his shoulders. She'd probably drawn blood, but he didn't care. As her sheath contracted around his cock, that sent him over, and he flooded her with his own release. He kissed her wildly, his tongue tangling with hers as they came together, their mutual orgasms sending them both into a tailspin of pleasure.

The words *I love you* flashed in his head, and he almost blurted them out. But he bit his tongue, not wanting to ruin this moment. He didn't know if he could love someone else again. But as he withdrew from her and she kissed him so sweetly, his heart clenched despite himself.

They righted their clothing, laughing a little, and Gavin took her to a nearby bench so they could catch their breath. Sweat had beaded on their foreheads despite the cool weather. He went inside the vineyard's main building to fetch them bottles of water, and he handed her one with a smile. "Don't want to get dehydrated," he said by way of explanation.

She rolled her eyes. "Thank you, I think." She lifted the bottle and took a long drink, her throat moving as she swallowed. "Most guys just like to spoon, but I think this is the best after-sex gift I've ever gotten."

He grinned. "Told you you'd get thirsty."

After they had drunk their fill, Kat leaned against his shoulder, and he placed an arm around her. He knew this little idyll couldn't last, but he stupidly hoped it would. Those treacherous words filled his mind again—*I love you*—but he refused to let them free.

God, he'd never acted like this before. He'd only ever had sex in a bed, yet with Kat, he couldn't control himself. The scariest part was that it wasn't just that he desired her: it was that he wanted to be with her every hour of every day.

In a world all his own, he didn't hear Kat's words at first. "What did you say?"

"I asked what we're doing." She sat up so she could look him in the eye. "Or more specifically, what do *you* think it is?"

He rubbed a hand against his beard. He wasn't stupid enough not to know what a potential minefield that question was. He weighed the pros and cons of honesty versus softening the blow. Remembering their conversation last night—about how Kat didn't want to be some "rebound chick"—he finally replied, "I don't know."

She huffed out a breath. "That's not an answer."

"It's as much an answer as I can give right now. Do you want me to lie and say I want to spend the rest of my life with you? Because I don't know if that's the case or not."

His heart told him he was a liar, but he told his heart to shut up. Images of Teagan and his broken marriage were enough of a reason to keep his distance.

"So we're just having an affair?"

"No!" He stood up to pace, and Kat watched him with wary eyes. "It's not just a fling to me. And I know it isn't for you, either."

"Common sense tells me that a relationship built only on sex is just that: a fling." She crossed her arms over her breasts, and then she let out a sigh. "I keep telling myself this is a bad idea, but I can't stay away from you. It's like some compulsion."

He barked out a laugh. "I'm not sure that's a compliment."

"It wasn't supposed to be. But I'm also not going to lie and say we don't have something more between us than sexual attraction." When he didn't deny it, she just nodded. "I'm scared too, Gavin," she whispered.

The word *scared* was like a thorn in his heart, and it

stabbed him, over and over again. "This doesn't have anything to do with being scared."

"Doesn't it?"

"No, it doesn't. I'm just trying to keep you safe. Don't you get it? I'm poison. My wife almost died and I couldn't save her from that. How can I have another relationship without repeating the same mistake?"

Kat covered her mouth, and he realized he hadn't told her about Teagan overdosing. But he needed her to understand. In a ragged voice, he said, "Teagan tried to kill herself. She overdosed on painkillers, and Emma found her on the bathroom floor. We didn't know if she'd survive the night." All he could see now was Teagan, the ambulance, the paramedics, his daughter's dry eyes. "She was sick for so long and I tried to get her help. I tried to get her to take her meds. Hell, I threatened divorce every time she decided she didn't need her meds anymore. I told her I'd take Emma and run. I made ultimatum after ultimatum; I hid the pills she'd get from ten different doctors."

Kat got up and touched him on the arm. "You can't blame yourself, Gavin. You can't."

"Of course I can. She was my responsibility, when she got so bad she couldn't take care of herself. But I failed her, and I failed Emma." He gripped her forearms, because he had to make her see. "I will not be the cause of another woman's downfall. I won't watch as she gets sicker and sicker and everything falls apart." He practically growled the next words, and he knew he was gripping her arms too tightly. But she didn't even flinch. "Do you get it now, Kat?"

Her eyes glimmered with tears, but they didn't fall. "I get it," she breathed. "I get that you blame yourself, because you think you have to save everyone. You can't save everyone, Gavin." She smiled, a smile so sad that it tore him apart. "Now you're throwing away what could be because of that fear."

She finally pulled away, and he let her go. He didn't want to let her go, but he knew without a doubt that he had to.

"I'm sorry," he said to her back.

She sniffled, turning to look over her shoulder at him. "If you were really sorry, or really wanted things to be different, you would make them happen." He flinched as she turned to face him once again. "I know what it's like to lose people, Gavin. I've been alone for so much of my life that it's almost second nature, but I also know when I'm screwing myself over for no reason. And that's what you're doing—to me, and to yourself."

"Kat…"

"I hope you figure things out. I really do." She kissed him on the cheek before she walked away.

CHAPTER THIRTEEN

Kat didn't know where she would go now. She couldn't go back to Gavin's apartment, could she? She drove to Lillian's place, ignoring the boarded-up window and the police tape left behind in some spots. A police car sat parked some yards away, always on watch. At least she wouldn't be completely alone.

The house seemed especially lonely tonight. She flipped on a light and wandered through the house, stopping in her grandmother's room. She found herself crawling onto the bed that was covered in a quilt Lillian had sewn some years ago when her eyesight had still been good, and Kat inhaled its scent: lavender and Bengay. She smiled. She missed her grandmother fiercely, and especially on a day like today, when she could've used her frank advice.

You can't help men from being stupid, she would say. *They were born stupid. All you can do is hope they figure it out before you end up six feet under.* Then she would've made Kat homemade macaroni and cheese with freshly baked bread and filled her up with so many carbohydrates that there was no way she could think about any guy for at least twenty-four hours.

She rubbed a hand against the quilt, tracing the stitches. Would Lillian have liked Gavin? She wanted to believe she would have, although she probably would've threatened to take him over her knee for his behavior. Kat couldn't help the laugh that burst from her when she imagined such a sight.

The doorbell rang, and Kat's heart pounded, thinking the worst. But when she opened the door, it wasn't a police officer or some angry gamer at her doorstep, but Grace Danvers instead.

"Hey there," she said. "I was on my way to Jaime's and wondered if you'd like to have dinner tonight? He's cooking, so I promise it'll be worth your while."

Kat narrowed her eyes. "Did Gavin send you?"

"Not exactly. But we ran into him and he was even grumpier than usual, and I put two and two together." Grace's eyes softened. "Are you okay?"

The tears that Kat had held back threatened to come, but she swallowed and forced them away. "I will be," she murmured. "And dinner sounds great."

The two women arrived at Jaime's—and now Grace's—place only to be greeted with the sound of him yelling something in Spanish.

Kat raised an eyebrow. "Everything okay in there?"

"I can never understand him when he gets pissed." Grace entered the kitchen, and Kat sat down in the living room, smiling as she listened to them talking.

"Are you yelling at the oven?" Grace asked, amusement lacing her voice.

"Yes, because it never *fucking works.*" Kat heard Jaime mutter something, and then Grace laughed.

She popped her head around the corner to say to Kat, "Everything's fine. Jaime's just being a drama king."

"I am not a drama king!"

"Yes, you are. Accept it. I've never seen anyone be as dramatic about cooking as you."

"I'm not dramatic. I'm passionate."

Their voices turned to murmurs once again, and Kat could make out a giggle and then what were probably noises signaling kissing of some sort. She sighed. She appreciated that Grace had thought to invite her so she wouldn't be alone tonight, but she wasn't sure she had the juice to watch a happy couple being happy.

Kat was grateful when Jaime and Grace made a point to include her in the conversation, even when she fell silent and melancholy. She knew too many couples who would simply talk to each other if the third party wasn't entertaining, and although Kat didn't feel like talking much, she couldn't fault them for trying.

"How's everything at the school?" Jaime served himself some stuffed peppers. Handsome and talented, Jaime was the type of guy Kat would normally go for, but ever since he'd laid eyes on Grace Danvers, he'd been in love with her, and Grace with him. Although Grace had admitted to her that Jaime had taken a while to realize he loved her, which only reminded her of another man who seemed incapable of being honest.

Don't think about Gavin, she told herself sternly.

"School's good. I'm looking forward to Thanksgiving break, though."

Jaime laughed. "Already?"

"Weren't you just talking about how you couldn't wait for the holidays?" Grace eyed him over her water glass. "I think your exact words were, 'if I have to spend one more day with these interns…'"

He waved a hand. "That's different. She gets to work with cute kids. I have to work with annoying twenty-one-year-olds. They think they know everything already."

"Like you weren't the same at that age," Grace countered.

"Weren't we all?" Kat smiled, thinking about how she thought she'd known everything back then, too. It was hard to believe it had been six years ago—it seemed both forever ago and just yesterday.

"Graciela here definitely was." At her outraged gasp, Jaime laughed. "I remember a certain girl telling me that I was totally wrong about when blueberries were in season." He looked at Kat as he continued. "Here I was, the executive chef, making all kinds of strides, and in comes this not-yet-graduated college student, looking all sweet and docile, and she pipes up and tells me I'm wrong about this one thing, to the point that she brings me three articles to prove she's right later in the day."

By this point, Grace was blushing so red that her entire face was aflame. "Do you have to remind us all?"

He smiled at his fiancée, which just earned him a scowl. "But you were so cute."

The rest of the evening was taken up with Grace and Jaime bantering and Kat teasing them both as much as she could, but by the time they drifted to the living room to watch TV, Kat was content with just watching those two lovebirds coo at each other. Grace curled up on Jaime's lap like a golden kitten, and he wrapped his arms around her as they watched

TV. Kat took a spot on the couch opposite, munching on left-over empanadas de leche that were so delicious, she could've eaten an entire bowlful. Made of fried plantains stuffed with vanilla custard, the dessert hit just the spot for Kat's broken heart.

When Jaime left to take a call, Grace got up to sit next to Kat.

"Now we're alone," she said in a conspiratorial whisper. "His parents always talk forever, so we have some time."

Kat swallowed the last bite of empanada. "Time for what?"

"Something's happened between you and my brother."

She wanted to make a joke about not being interested in Adam, but her heart wasn't in it. Sighing, she replied, "There's not much to tell." Nothing that she'd tell his sister, anyway.

"You were staying at Gavin's place during all this, but then I meet him today and he looked like he could murder anyone who looked at him sideways. Then I find you returning home even though there haven't been any suspects found, looking so exhausted that I know something's up." Grace paused. "Of course, you don't have to tell me anything, but I'm worried about you. About the both of you."

Those tears that Kat had held back threatened again. She took a deep breath. "If there was anything between us, it's over now."

"Oh, Kat." Grace rubbed her arm.

"The thing is, I knew he wasn't ready. But I pushed him anyway, and now I'm here, about to cry again over the stupid man." Kat sniffled, wiping at her eyes underneath her glasses. "I have half a mind to run him over with a tractor."

"I'm sure he deserves it." Grace made soothing noises, rather like a mother hen, and Kat let herself be taken care of for once. In a halting voice, Grace then asked, "Did he tell you anything about him and Teagan?"

Kat nodded. "I had no idea that she tried to commit suicide. I knew she wasn't well, but to go that far…"

"He took it really hard, and so did Emma. I know he blames himself for everything Teagan went through, but especially for her overdosing."

"How can he blame himself? He did all he could."

Grace shrugged, her face sad. "We know that, but he's always been the one who feels like he has to save people. Sometimes I wonder if he didn't fall in love with Teagan because he sensed she needed saving. She wasn't always sick, but there were signs, even when they were younger." She sighed. "I was too young to really notice, plus Adam's wife Carolyn was in the accident, and it all kind of merged together. Now that I think about it, though, it makes a twisted kind of sense."

All the food Kat had just eaten now sat like a rock in her stomach. She could've laughed at everything Grace was saying: how was it that two people who were so similar like she and Gavin would've found each other? Taking on the world's burdens while forgetting about taking care of themselves. It was a selfish kind of selflessness, Kat reflected, her head starting to pound.

"Do you love him?"

Kat stared at Grace. The young woman just waited, her gaze neither judging nor pitying. When Kat couldn't find the words to respond, she knew the answer immediately: she loved him. She did. She didn't know when it had happened, but despite everything, she'd fallen in love with Gavin.

Grace smiled sadly, as if she could sense Kat's inner

thoughts. "I hope you fight for him, Kat," she said quietly. "He's been so lonely, and I've never seen him as happy as he has been lately. I know that's because of you. And I bet you everything he loves you, too."

Kat gulped back a sob, but she couldn't stop the tears. Not this time. Unlike the tears she'd shed at Gavin's, these tears were silent. She sat and let the tears flow down her cheeks, dripping from her chin, and she didn't try to stop them. Grace sat with her and let her cry, handing her a tissue here and there, murmuring words that Kat didn't register but appreciated nonetheless.

I love him, she kept repeating to herself, and her heart cracked for the thousandth time. *I love him, and he's too stubborn to let me.*

"For what it's worth," Grace said, "he's an idiot. A giant, blithering idiot. He and Adam could form a club for stupid brothers. I'm tempted to call Joy just to have her tell you all the stupid things Adam did before he figured things out."

Kat sniffled, laughing a little. "It must be genetic."

"My dad is just as stubborn. He could give both Adam and Gavin a run for their money." Grace rolled her eyes.

"I don't know what to do." Kat hated to admit that, but it was true. The stubborn part of her wanted to get Gavin to see sense, while the scared part of her wanted to hide underground until things returned to normal.

"Yes, you do. Or, you will. If there's anyone who can figure this out, it's you." Grace smiled. "You're way too smart not to find a way to get Gavin to take his head out of his ass."

The evening wound down after that, and Kat knew she needed to go home and be by herself for a while. Although

Grace said she could stay with them, Kat was tired of not sleeping in her own bed.

"I'll be fine," she reassured them. "The police are watching the house."

Grace made a face, but she didn't argue. Jaime pressed a kiss to her temple before murmuring something in her ear.

When Kat arrived back at the house, she could almost imagine nothing had happened in the last few weeks. She couldn't see the boarded-up window in the darkness, and although she knew one of the police officers was nearby, she liked to imagine it was just any other car parked instead.

Right before she got into bed, her phone sounded with a text. *Everything okay?* the message read, and her heart clenched when she saw that it was from Gavin.

She was half-tempted not to respond, but then he'd just worry himself to death. She sent off a quick reply—*Everything's fine*—before turning off her lamp and trying to go to sleep.

But a few minutes later, Gavin sent her one last message: *I'm sorry, Kat.*

She didn't respond. She turned her phone on silent and closed her eyes, but all she could see was Gavin's face and his voice saying those very words, and it was all she could think about for some hours to come.

CHAPTER FOURTEEN

Gavin had been in a bad mood for days. The worst part of it was that he was well aware that it was his own fault, so he walked around with a metaphorical cloud over his head, constantly raining down on him. Despite his best efforts, Emma noticed and asked him what was wrong, but how could he tell his daughter what had happened with him and Kat? So he'd told her it was just the gloomy weather and left it at that, although his daughter was way too perceptive to take him at his word.

The weekend before Halloween consisted of getting River's Bend ready for its Halloween festivities. The vineyard hadn't done much in the way of celebrating in the last few years, but with the good harvest this year, Adam had decided they should celebrate as much as possible. When Gavin entered the vineyard's main building, the entire front room was decorated with pumpkins and gourds, bats and skeletons, and he had to wave away fake cobwebs to get to Adam's office in the back.

"He's not in yet!" Kerry, the front desk woman and Adam's

assistant, called to him. "But he should be back in the next half hour."

Gavin grunted and sat down on one of the chairs to wait for his brother. He only wanted to pick up his paycheck; he wondered if he could just get it from Adam's office and tell his brother later that he'd been in a hurry. Then again, after all the financial troubles River's Bend had gone through, including one of the interns embezzling funds, taking a paycheck was probably not in Gavin's best interests.

The vineyard bustled with activity. Jaime was planning some extravagant Halloween menu, and they were debuting a new type of wine as well. Gavin was glad that things were turning around for the business, but he'd never wanted to be a part of the frenzy the vineyard tended to create in his family. When Gavin was a kid, Carl Danvers had considered River's Bend his fourth child, and oftentimes neglected his own family to tend to it. While Adam had worked to take it over, Gavin had done his best to avoid having to deal with the vineyard whatsoever. He'd never wanted to be in Carl's shadow, unlike his brother.

"Gavin, are you looking for me?" Adam walked up to him. "Sorry if I made you wait."

Gavin shrugged as he got up. "I just need my paycheck."

"Sure thing." Adam waved at him to follow, and Gavin went back into Adam's office, which had also been decorated with various Halloween items. He had a feeling Adam hadn't been the one to hang bats overhead or place a full-size skeleton on one of the chairs opposite his desk.

Gavin poked the skeleton. "Joy do this?"

"Yes, and if you mess up that skeleton, she'll kill us both and turn us into skeletons to put on display." Adam rifled through the documents on his desk to pull out a check. Gavin wasn't entirely sure why the vineyard didn't allow employees direct deposit, but more than likely, it was one of Adam's random rules that kept them in the Stone Age in terms of payment systems.

As Gavin turned to go, Adam asked, "How are you, by the way?"

He did not want to have this conversation. He shrugged, looking everywhere but at his brother. "Same as always."

"Which means what, exactly?" When Gavin didn't reply, Adam sighed. "I know that something happened with you and Kat. Grace was pissed at you and told me she'd 'kick you in the kneecap' the next time she saw you. Considering our sister isn't prone to violence, that makes me think something is up."

Did his entire family have to get involved in his love life? He and Kat had slept together—twice—but now it was over. Couldn't everyone just leave it alone?

"We had a misunderstanding," Gavin ground out, "but it's over. Now, if you're done interrogating me, I need to get back to work."

"I know you don't like talking about how you feel. Hell, neither do I, but I know you haven't been the same since everything with Teagan." Adam lowered his voice. "You can't keep it all locked inside. I tried it with Carolyn, and I almost lost Joy because of it."

Old resentments surfaced with surprising force: how Adam hadn't been there when Gavin's marriage was falling apart. How he'd felt like his brother had never been interested in anything but this stupid vineyard. He knew very well he was being petty and selfish, but that knowledge wasn't enough to keep him from saying, "It's none of your business. Don't try to act like you care now."

Adam reared back, before his eyes darkened with anger. "What the hell does that mean?"

"It means that you weren't exactly interested when Teagan was losing her damn mind, when she almost killed herself. Where were you then? I don't remember you giving me advice then."

Adam just stared at Gavin, the blood draining from his face. A twinge of guilt pricked at Gavin's gut, but he ignored it. "That's what I thought. Now, like I said, I have work to do."

"I know I wasn't there," Adam said quietly. "I didn't know what to say. I was still so broken up about Carolyn that I didn't know how I could help. But I did call, Gavin. I was worried about you, and still am." He swallowed. "You're my brother—for better or for worse."

For some reason, Adam's quiet only enraged Gavin further. His anger about Teagan, about Kat, about Emma, about his entire family, exploded inside of his chest like a bomb that had been ticking for years. "Don't act like you really tried," he hissed. "I needed you, and you weren't there." His breathing became ragged, and he wished he could just punch a wall. "I watched my wife almost die and you didn't care!"

"My own wife died!" Adam yelled. "She died and I had to figure out how to live without her. I had to watch as they lowered her into the ground in that casket, knowing I would never hear her voice or touch her again. So don't talk to me about loss! Don't act like you're the only one who's suffered."

"At least I came back for the funeral! Would you have come if Teagan had died?"

They were shouting now, but neither seemed to care. "What the fuck kind of question is that? Jesus, Gavin, do you hate me that much?"

They continued yelling, until Jaime burst into the office, swearing at them both. "The fuck are you two doing?" he demanded. "Everyone in the entire town can hear you screaming at each other." When he saw that they were close to blows, he pushed them apart with a curse. "Get it together, you two."

Gavin wrenched away from Jaime's grasp. "I'm leaving," he muttered.

"Good, go home and cool off." Jaime turned to Adam. "And you should probably do the same."

Gavin didn't hear what Adam said in reply. He stalked out of the vineyard and climbed into his truck, driving off without caring that he still had work to do. Anger roiled through him and his vision was a haze of red. He couldn't throttle his own brother. Adam didn't get it; he didn't understand how Gavin had had to shoulder everything by himself. Adam had had their parents, Grace, the entire town of Heron's Landing when Carolyn had died. But Gavin had had no one.

When he arrived back at his apartment, he pressed his forehead to the steering wheel. As his anger drained away and became exhaustion, a small voice inside of his head told him that his family had reached out to him, but he'd pushed them away. He'd told them he'd take care of everything. He hadn't wanted their help. But that immature part of his soul had wished they'd fought for him anyway. That they'd tried one more time, as opposed to giving up so easily.

Entering the apartment, he saw a bright scrap of silk

underneath his pillow in his bedroom, and pulling it out, he realized it was Kat's headscarf. He inhaled it, and her scent enveloped him. He remembered how they'd made love in this very bed, and how she'd looked at him when he'd touched her.

You can't keep it all locked inside. I tried it with Carolyn, and I almost lost Joy because of it.

Gavin sat down on the bed, clutching the headscarf. He knew with a painful kind of clarity that despite his anger at his brother, Adam had spoken a truth that resonated in Gavin's soul. He had been keeping it all locked inside, and in his fear of being vulnerable a second time, he'd pushed Kat away. He'd pushed her away because loving her was terrifying.

He groaned. God, he was a fool, a coward, the type of man who didn't deserve a woman as amazing as Kat. He'd told her she deserved better than his broken self, but that was only because he hadn't tried to mend his own heart. He'd kept his heart broken and battered, its own kind of shield from the terrors of the world. And Teagan had been the perfect excuse, hadn't she?

Gavin dragged his fingers through his hair. He didn't know if he could get Kat back, but he had to at least tell her he loved her. He didn't expect her to forgive him, but he could fight for her. He would fight for her to the ends of the earth.

He stuffed the headscarf into his pocket for good luck, resolving to find Kat that very afternoon and tell her how sorry he was. Then he grimaced, knowing he'd need to apologize to Adam as well. He'd really fucked things up, hadn't he?

But Kat was at work right now, and he had no idea when she'd be home. He was halfway tempted to sit on her doorstep and wait for her, but given everything that had happened at her grandmother's place, that probably wasn't the best plan. Besides, he needed to be home when Emma got off the bus.

As he was debating, his phone rang. To his shock, Kat's number flashed on the screen.

"Kat? Are you okay?" His heart pounded wildly, imagining all sorts of things that could've happened now.

"I'm fine. Gavin, Emma's missing."

CHAPTER FIFTEEN

K at tried her best to throw herself into her work. She couldn't let her heartbreak over Gavin keep her from being a good teacher. But her students were certainly old enough to have heard about her house being vandalized, and being just kids, she had to volley tons of questions every single class.

Finally, it go to the point that Kat made a blanket rule that if anyone talked about the subject, they'd get a demerit. That had nipped the discussion in the bud—at least when Kat was present. She obviously had no power to keep the kids from talking about it when she wasn't around.

Two weeks after Gavin had broken her heart, Kat was grateful that there hadn't been any more threats against her. The police hadn't found any leads despite their best efforts, though. Kat had a feeling, being such a tiny police force, that they didn't exactly have the capability to track down somebody like this. And now that the threats seemed to be stopping, there wasn't as much focus on it as before.

On Wednesday, Kat had a longer lunch break and decided

to go out to eat. It was chilly but the sky was clear, and she enjoyed looking at the autumn leaves. It was only a short drive to the town's Main Street and to Trudy's Diner. There were a few regulars at their booths, but since it was the middle of the week, it wasn't busy. Kat found her favorite booth. She didn't even look at a menu: she always got the same thing from Trudy's.

"The usual?" said the waitress, Leslie, with a warm smile.

"Yeah, but let's do a chocolate shake instead of strawberry."

"You got it." Leslie winked.

Normally, Kat would've asked Leslie about her kids, how her knee was doing after her recent surgery, and other small talk. Today, though, Kat wanted to sit by herself and not talk for a second. It didn't help that everything in this town reminded her of Gavin. That was the worst thing about small towns: you couldn't disappear inside them when you really wanted to.

Kat soon had her cheeseburger, fries, and chocolate shake to work on. She dipped her fries in the shake in between bites of her burger.

"I didn't know anyone really did that," said a familiar voice. Silas smiled at her, and then gestured at the empty seat across from her. "Can I join you?"

Kat had barely spoken to Silas since he'd told her to watch herself with Gavin. Before that, Silas had stopped by Gavin's more than once to check on her, but the meetings had ended after that weird conversation at school.

At the moment, she was tempted to tell him she was in a hurry, but instead, she found herself falling back to her usual polite self. Apparently Midwestern politeness had rubbed off on her since moving here.

"Sure," she said without enthusiasm.

Silas slid into the booth and grabbed a fry from her plate. "I'm starving."

"Then you should order something." Kat wasn't about to share her fries along with her company. She had her limits.

Silas snagged another fry, clearly enjoying her annoyance. "I had no idea you hated sharing food."

"I don't. Just French fries."

"Sure, okay."

Silas ordered his lunch and proceeded to watch Kat eat. She tried to come up with something to say, but her brain just couldn't find the words. Besides, Silas had invited himself to sit with her: he could start the conversation. *Apparently I'm extra petty when I'm grumpy,* she thought wryly.

"How are you doing? I feel like we don't talk anymore." Silas's expression was sad.

Kat instantly felt guilty. Silas was a little strange, but he didn't mean any harm. She gave him a halfhearted smile. "I'm sorry. I've just been busy."

Silas traced an invisible line on the tabletop. "I was afraid of this, you know. This always happens when my female friends start dating somebody." He didn't look up at her, but instead watched his own finger. "The boyfriend always gets jealous of me."

Kat blinked at him. "Gavin isn't my boyfriend." *He's not my anything now,* she thought morosely.

"He's not?" Silas's gaze shot to hers.

"I mean, we're not official." It was true-ish.

"Oh. Well. My point still stands."

Silas's grilled cheese and tomato soup arrived. He tore off

a piece of his sandwich and watched the cheese stretch. "Look at that. Beautiful."

"Gavin has nothing to do with me being busy," she said.

Silas raised an eyebrow in obvious disbelief.

Kat found herself blushing. "I mean, he isn't the reason I haven't been available lately. That's my fault and my fault only. Gavin doesn't dictate who I get to hang out with."

Silas's face closed. "So you're saying you're avoiding me because you don't want to talk to me."

"I mean, what you said to me about having to watch myself with Gavin…" She shook her head. "You keep saying he's going to hurt me or something. And he's never hurt me—"

She stopped, because he *had* hurt her. He'd pushed her away. Maybe that hadn't been what Silas had been warning her about, but he hadn't been wrong, either.

Silas reached out and touched her hand. "I'm just worried about you. Can't we be friends again?"

"I don't know," she answered honestly.

His fingers closed around her hand. "That's not fair, and you know it."

"I'm just trying to be honest."

"You haven't been honest this entire conversation." His fingers dug into her hand to the point that she felt the bite of his fingernails. Then just as suddenly, he let her hand go.

"I think I'll take this to-go." He got up and grabbed one of the to-go containers, sloshing almost half of his tomato soup onto the table. "See you around, Kat."

After Silas had left, Leslie wiped up the spilled soup. "Goodness, he had a bee in his bonnet, didn't he?"

Kat felt her burger and fries congeal in her stomach. "I should get back to school."

Leslie looked more closely at Kat's face. "You okay, honey? You're looking pale. Are you coming down with something?"

"I just—I need to go."

Inside her car, Kat forced herself to take deep breaths. She didn't know what was up with Silas, but something in her gut told her to stay away from him.

Gavin isn't the man I have to watch out for.

ON A BLUSTERY FRIDAY BEFORE HALLOWEEN, Kat was trying to keep her kids from completely losing focus. They were excited about dressing up and going trick-or-treating, not to mention comparing their costume ideas with the other kids'. When one boy found out another was also going as Captain America, you would've thought it had been revealed the first boy had murdered the other's puppy.

As Kat took role, she realized that Emma wasn't in class. She frowned. Mrs. Gentry hadn't mentioned that Emma was absent today, but maybe she'd forgotten. Everyone seemed to be distracted today. But something niggled in the back of Kat's mind. She sent a text message to Mrs. Gentry. *Is Emma Danvers sick today?*

Mrs. Gentry messaged back immediately. *No, why? Is she not in computer class?*

Kat felt ice drip down her spine. Was Emma hiding somewhere again? But Kat couldn't leave her kids, so she sent another message to Mrs. Gentry and asked her to begin looking for Emma.

By the end of her class, Kat was a bundle of nerves. Mrs.

Gentry came up to her and said in a low voice, "Go tell Principal Layton. Now."

That meant Mrs. Gentry hadn't found Emma. Kat walked as quickly as she could without alerting suspicion, her heart pounding in her chest. She checked the closet where Emma had hidden before, but it was locked. Although there was no way the girl could've gotten a key, Kat knocked on the door anyway.

"Emma, are you in there?"

Silence. Where could she have gone?

Outside, the wind was blowing harder, and it was starting to rain. She needed to call Gavin. Maybe he knew where she could've gone.

Kat did her best to stave off panic. Panic wouldn't help find Emma. She had to keep a clear head, even when her heart was about to pound right out of her chest. By the time she got to Principal Layton's office and told her that Emma Danvers was missing, Kat's panic had turned into resolve.

Gavin might've broken her heart, but she was not going to let them go through another tragedy. He'd already almost lost his first wife. The thought that something would happen to his daughter? It was unthinkable.

"Do you have any idea where she could be?" Principal Layton said hurriedly as she dialed the police. "Did you look in the closets?"

"Yes. They're all locked. I don't see how she could've gotten inside them."

"I have a skeleton key: I'll check them."

"Someone needs to inform her father," said Kat quietly.

Principal Layton nodded tightly. "I'll do that once I get off the phone with the police. If you find her, call my cell phone." She handed Kat a Post-it with her cell phone number on it.

Kat realized she'd left her own phone in the computer room. As she grabbed her things, thankful she didn't have another class to teach that afternoon, Silas stepped inside the room.

"I ran into Jenny," he said, referring to Mrs. Gentry. "Any idea where Emma is?"

Kat checked her coat: purse, keys, phone. Hat. She'd brought a hat—right? She dug around in her bag and found her hat at the bottom.

"No, no idea," she said in a rush. "I'm going to go looking for her now."

Silas's face creased. "Kat, it's raining. You shouldn't go out there."

Kat didn't have time to argue. "I need to go. I'm going to keep looking in the school first before I go outside." A few months ago, she would've invited Silas to come along, but since he'd been so weird with her staying with Gavin, an awkwardness had formed between them.

"I'll help. Tell me where to go."

Kat instantly felt guilty for not including Silas, who just wanted to help. She shouldn't let personal matters get in the way of finding Emma. "I'm going to search the first floor. Principal Layton has a key to open the janitorial closets, if she somehow got into one. How about you search down here?"

"Will do." Silas touched Kat's arm, squeezing it. "We'll find her. Don't worry."

Kat met up with Principal Layton and they split up to cover more of the school. The police were on their way, although Principal Layton had told them to keep things on the down-low so as to not upset the other students. Kat had a feeling Principal Layton wanted to avoid any parents finding out before it was necessary. There was no need to create an entire panic throughout the community.

Kat and Principal Layton—Linda, as she'd insisted Kat call her—began to open one closet after the other. Considering the school was hardly huge, it didn't take long to see that Emma wasn't hiding in any of them. Inside the closet she'd hidden in earlier in the school year, Kat pushed aside a mop and lifted up a bucket, as if the young girl could've hidden underneath it like some woodland creature.

"How could she have run away without anyone noticing?" Linda's voice was low and anguished. "And where are the police? It's been fifteen minutes."

"What about an Amber alert?" said Kat. "Would that help?"

"I'm not sure if this would count—yet." Linda rubbed her temples. "Let's look in the classrooms that aren't in use."

Linda unlocked the few classrooms that were mostly for storage—old books, desks, chairs filled one room almost to the ceiling—but no Emma. Right then, the wind started blowing so hard that Kat could hear it whistling from inside the school.

Emma had been doing so much better lately, but something must've triggered her into hiding. Kat just prayed that nothing more sinister had happened this time. If Emma had been taken, or was hurt... Gavin wouldn't survive, she knew that much.

"Wait, did you call Gavin—I mean, Mr. Danvers?" said Kat to Linda.

Linda swore, words that Kat rarely heard at the elementary school. "No. Shit. I was too preoccupied with the police and then I wanted to find you--"

Kat didn't wait for her to explain further. "I've got this. I'll meet up with you in a second."

Kat's heart pounded as she called Gavin. When he didn't pick up for a long second, she prayed under her breath that he wouldn't ignore her call.

When he finally answered, she could've sobbed with relief.

"Gavin," she said in a shaky voice, "Emma is missing."

CHAPTER SIXTEEN

Gavin had never driven so fast in his entire life. He gripped the steering wheel with white knuckles, praying and begging anyone listening to keep his daughter safe.

Emma had to be safe. She was most likely hiding somewhere, and they just hadn't found her yet. Rage at the school bubbled over, and he didn't realize he'd accelerated until he almost ran himself off of the road. He forced himself to slow down, even as it felt like hours before he'd reach the school when it was only across town.

After Gavin had left River's Bend, Adam had assured him that he'd follow behind him as soon as he found Joy so she could help in the search. Gavin had hardly listened to his brother. Adam could bring the entire family if he wanted, but Gavin wasn't about to wait around for them all, either.

How had the school lost his daughter? *Again?* He wanted to throttle someone. He wanted to demand why everyone at that damn school couldn't keep track of one little girl. If she had gotten hurt, or worse…

He took a deep breath. Then another. The panic he'd felt when he'd found Teagan on the bathroom floor. He hated feeling this helpless, and he couldn't understand how the past seemed to be repeating itself.

Before he went to the school, he planned to check the apartment. The school was about three miles from home, so although it would be a long walk, it wasn't an insane thing to think Emma might go home. Gavin had told her about the spare key in the flower pot next to the front door. She could get inside, at least.

At a stoplight, Gavin texted Kat and Adam to let them know he'd be stopping by the apartment first.

The second Gavin put the car in park, he jumped out and jogged to the apartment. Before he went inside, he lifted up the flowerpot: the key was there. *Maybe she put it back after using it.*

"Emma? Are you in here?" he said as he opened the front door. Despite it still being daylight, the storm rolling in made the apartment especially dark. Gavin flipped on a lamp, saying a second time, "Emma? If you're here, I'm not mad. I just want to make sure you're okay."

No answer. His heart fell. Even though he knew she wasn't here, he looked in her room. He looked in the tiny kitchen, where he and Kat had made dinner. He even looked in the bathroom, pulling the shower curtain aside.

He returned to Emma's room and sat down on her bed. He brushed his palm across her bedspread, the cloth bright pink and covered in purple stars and unicorns. She had a sparkly throw pillow that Gavin had recently bought for her after much begging. He felt his throat close.

He had to get up. He had to find his daughter. Yet it was

like his body was frozen. He didn't even know how he was still breathing.

On Emma's nightstand was a picture frame. Gavin picked it up, looking at the photo of Teagan and Emma.

Teagan. Shit. He needed to call her. He closed his eyes.

How could he tell Teagan he didn't know where their daughter was? The news could send her into another breakdown. She was recovering and in a much better place, but she was still fragile.

He brushed his thumb over Emma's face in the photograph. He had to find her. There was no other choice.

As Gavin returned to his car, he dialed Teagan's number. He hated that he'd put her into a panic, but after he'd talked to her about Emma hiding in a closet last time, she'd told him in no uncertain terms to call her if it happened again. *I want to know what's going on with my daughter*, she'd said, so reasonably that Gavin could hardly say no.

He called Teagan and hoped she wouldn't pick up. But she did, and he wished he'd thought of what to tell her beforehand.

Before she could even greet him, he said bluntly, "Emma is missing from school."

He heard a sharp intake of breath on the other end. "For how long?" Teagan finally asked.

"I don't know. An hour? Two? Kat—Miss Williamson—called to tell me. I'm driving over to the school right now." Gavin told Teagan the little information that he'd gotten from Kat before getting into his car.

"We're going to find her," he said, almost trying to convince himself as much as Teagan.

"Oh God, Gavin. Are you sure? Is she at home somehow? Maybe she walked there? Have you checked there?"

"I just checked. There was no sign of her."

"How did no one see her leave? She's a little kid! What kind of school loses a student?"

Gavin could feel Teagan's anger radiating through the phone. He felt the same way: he wanted heads to roll. But he couldn't give into the anger. Not yet.

"I don't know. But I'll find her. I'll do whatever it takes."

Gavin heard Teagan moving in the background. "I can get a plane ticket to Missouri. If I leave treatment voluntarily I can't come back, but—"

"No, don't do that." He gentled his tone. "You need to stay where you are. By the time you get here, we'll have found her."

"What if you don't? I'm her mother." Teagan started crying. "I'm her mother, and I'm not even there to look for her."

Gavin felt the weight of the world on his shoulders right then. As he stopped at a red light, he pressed his forehead to the steering wheel. He wished Teagan were here, that she could fly in right now and help with the search. Although they were no longer married, they were still friends and she was the mother of his child.

"I keep fucking everything up," he said hoarsely into the phone. "First you, now Emma."

Teagan was silent for a long moment. "What are you talking about? This is the school's fault, not yours."

"Does it matter? You almost died, Teagan. That was on my watch. I should've done more to help you, to get you into treatment. I was so convinced that you'd realize you needed help so I didn't push as hard as I could have. And look at what happened."

The light turned green right when Teagan replied, "You're an idiot, Gavin."

Gavin let out a rough laugh. "Yeah? Because I keep hurting people?"

"No, because you think you're in control of what other people do." Teagan sighed. "This isn't the time, but my mental health wasn't—and isn't—your fault. Maybe at the time I could've blamed you, but my brain was sick. It needed help, just like if I'd had cancer or a heart attack.

"Nothing you could've done would've kept me from going down into that dark place." Teagan's voice seemed to waver. "You didn't almost kill me, Gavin: you saved my life. You can't blame yourself for what happened."

Gavin felt like sobbing, but he was too numb. "Maybe, maybe not," he whispered. "But I can blame myself for our daughter running away. Or worse, getting kidnapped."

He finally pulled into the school parking lot, where police cars were lined up outside. Already he could see people from the town lined up outside.

"You'll find her. Because if you don't, Gavin Danvers, I'll kill you myself. I'll fly straight to Missouri and strangle you."

He let out a dark laugh. "I know you will."

Gavin was about to get out of his car when Teagan said, "Don't keep yourself walled up because you think you failed in our marriage. Neither of us failed. We did our best, but we got a shitty hand dealt to us. To me. And there's nothing we can do about it but move forward."

"When did you get so wise?"

"I've been in therapy for a while now. But the past doesn't matter now: finding our daughter is all that matters, okay? Focus on her. I'll do what I can from so far away." Gavin could hear the anguish in Teagan's voice. "Please keep me updated?"

After assuring Teagan that he or one of his family members would call her with any new information, Gavin looked through the crowd, trying to find Kat. When his gaze landed on her, he felt his heart constrict inside his chest.

Kat wasn't even Emma's mother, but here she was, searching for her. Helping and directing. Even after what had happened between them, after what he'd said to her. He'd hurt her badly, but she didn't hold that against him.

He didn't deserve Kat Williamson. But that didn't mean he could stop himself from wanting her.

I love her, he thought. It wasn't even surprising: it just made sense. He'd fallen in love with her kindness, her intelligence, her courage. She'd faced everything that had happened to her with a bravery that Gavin wished he could emulate. He truly admired her. And he wanted her all to himself.

God, he'd been an idiot. He'd pushed her away because he'd thought it was better off for *her*. He realized with a sinking feeling in his gut that in his attempt to be noble and self-sacrificing, he'd actually been arrogant and afraid. He'd hurt her because he'd been afraid of getting hurt again.

Gavin pressed through the crowd, but people kept stopping him to ask him questions. It meant a lot to him that this town he'd moved away from years ago still cared deeply about him and his daughter. But at the moment, he didn't want to answer questions from neighbors desperate for information he didn't have.

"Oh Gavin, we'll find her," said Leslie, her eyes filled with tears. "You know this entire town will turn itself upside down to find Emma."

Gavin forced himself to stop, to ignore Kat gazing at him from just yards away. His heart thumped hard in his chest. "I appreciate that," he ground out.

"She's so small. She couldn't have gotten that far," said Mike. He slapped Gavin on the shoulder. "Don't worry: she'll be found, safe and sound, and you'll look back at this with a chuckle."

Gavin doubted that, but he didn't feel inclined to argue. But the next person who told him he didn't need to worry was getting punched in the face. He forced himself to swallow his harsh words, saying thank you and nodding at whomever he walked past.

He focused on Kat. He focused on the woman who would be his pillar of strength in this insanity.

Yet even as he was about to enfold Kat in his arms, Adam and Joy came up to him and stopped him. Gavin almost growled at them in frustration. Kat sent him an amused glance.

"I can see by your face you haven't found her yet," said Adam gravely. "Do you have any idea where she could've gone?"

"People keep asking me the same damn question when I don't have any answers." Gavin wanted to yell, to fall to his knees and cry out in despair. The constant questions only made his agony worse.

Joy gently touched his arm. "We're all here for you. You're not in this alone."

Adam nodded. "Joy speaks the truth."

Gavin thought of his fight with Adam only an hour earlier. It seemed like it had happened a thousand years ago. He swallowed his pride and said, "Thank you. And I'm sorry I was a jackass to you. You didn't deserve it."

To Gavin's surprise, Adam wrapped his arms around him and gave him a quick, tight hug, pounding on his back. "It doesn't matter. All that matters is finding Emma. And anyway, we're brothers. We'll always be here for each other."

Kat had moved closer to the trio, and when Gavin finally was able to take in her beautiful face, her gentle eyes, he could barely restrain himself from collapsing into her arms.

"Hi," she said quietly. She took his hand and didn't let it go. "We'll find her, Gavin."

Despite having heard those words over and over, for whatever reason, he believed Kat this time. He squeezed her hand back, the lump in his throat too large now to say anything.

CHAPTER SEVENTEEN

Everything seemed to move at lightning speed after that. The police had already arrived by the time Kat had gotten off the phone with Gavin, and they were collecting any information before forming search parties.

With the school day ending, parents had begun to pick up their kids. When they saw the police presence, Principal Layton had done her best to explain the situation while the police had helped form search parties for everyone who wanted to help.

Next to the school was a large wooded area, about two acres wide. Kat had this feeling deep in her gut that Emma had disappeared into it. Why she'd run away, she didn't know. She just prayed they found the girl before it got dark—and before this storm broke.

"Have you seen Silas?" said Mrs. Gentry to Kat as they all waited for instructions.

Kat had completely forgotten about him. "No, not since earlier this afternoon. Why?"

Mrs. Gentry frowned. "He told me he'd find me near the south restrooms, but he never showed up."

"Weird. Maybe he was asked to help with searching the grounds?"

"Maybe."

Mrs. Gentry moved through the crowd, leaving Kat by herself. She did a halfhearted look around for Silas, but she didn't see him.

The second Kat laid eyes on Gavin when he arrived at the school, she forgot all about the missing Silas. Seeing Gavin, she wanted to throw her arms around him and hold him close. He looked wild-eyed, his face pale with terror. She'd never him look stricken like this. Her heart lurched inside her chest.

But they didn't have time to talk. After speaking with Kat, Gavin headed straight for Officer Haldon. He demanded updates, along with asking how many people they had organized to go search for Emma.

Kat interjected when needed, but she mostly just watched Gavin with a sense of awe and pride, while at the same time still hurting from his rejection. It was a strange mixture of emotions that she couldn't begin to unravel right then.

Rain began to patter down onto the pavement, and Kat lifted a hand to cover her hair. Gavin's expression turned grim.

"We have people looking in town, and down roads and streets, in case she's walking somewhere, along with the entire school grounds," said Officer Haldon to Gavin. "But we haven't found a trace of her."

"We need to search in the woods. Where's the search party for that?" said Gavin.

"I'm heading that one up myself." The young officer handed Gavin and then Kat a flashlight for the two of them, along with ponchos. "We need to move quickly. This storm is going to break, and it'll be dark soon."

Gavin didn't have to be told twice. Within moments, he and Kat were walking into the wooded area. Kat said a silent prayer of thanks that she'd worn her boots today. She put on the poncho and motioned to Gavin's.

"You're going to get wet," she said.

He gave her a strange look. "I guess." He put it on, but she had a feeling he didn't give a damn if he got soaking wet. And then got pneumonia for the trouble.

The search party fanned out, Gavin and Kat sticking together. Officer Haldon was the main point of contact, and if anyone found anything, they were to contact him immediately. Kat couldn't help but admire the young man's calm and efficiency in this situation. He'd managed to keep dozens of people from panicking and had put them to work.

The woods would've been pretty, if it weren't for the circumstances they found themselves in. The trees were bright with autumn colors, leaves crunching under their feet. The trees were big enough that although it was raining, it fell mostly on the treetops. The patter of rainfall soothed Kat's nerves.

"Emma! Emma!" Kat and Gavin shouted at the same time. Kat shivered as a cold wind blew through her sweater, and she looked up to see tiny snowflakes starting to fall. It was only supposed to rain, she thought in despair. What bad luck had brought them snow this early in the season?

At the moment, Gavin seemed mostly calm, but she knew it was just a façade. She could see how drawn his face was, how his voice broke whenever he called Emma's name. When they hadn't found her on the school grounds, he'd looked as if someone had shot him. Kat had almost expected him to slump to the ground, but he'd clenched his jaw and continued on. She knew he'd look for Emma for hours, days, weeks, if that was what it took. He'd never give up searching.

She could only pray they found her before the snow really started, and before it got dark, too.

Making him look into her eyes, she said with as much conviction as she could muster, "We're going to find her."

"She hates the dark," he whispered. "What if she had an episode and now she's trapped somewhere? She's only eight years old, Kat. She doesn't have her winter coat with her. She'll freeze to death."

"No, she won't, because we're going to find her. She's a smart girl. She could have already made it home, too. Maybe she was walking there all along." Kat tried to keep her tone hopeful, even though she couldn't believe her own words.

Joy had been appointed to stay at the apartment to make sure Emma didn't show up there, while Julia had returned to the Danvers house to watch for her there. Kat had a feeling that Emma was hiding somewhere and hadn't just walked out of school to go home early, but she still hoped she was wrong. If they got a call from Joy saying the girl was safe and sound, that was all that mattered.

She could hear other people calling and walking through the woods. The constant sound of the name *Emma* created an eerie kind of echo, like the forest itself were calling Emma's name. Gavin flashed his flashlight at shadowy recesses and under bushes. The further they walked into the woods, the more Kat's worry grew. They didn't have much time before it became dark.

"You were right," said Gavin suddenly. He stepped over a log before helping Kat over it.

Kat stared at him. "What?"

Gavin sighed, rubbing his forehead. "You were right. About everything. I knew Emma had some kind of illness, but I wanted to believe she wouldn't turn into her mother. Now she's run off because I'm such a stupid fool. If I hadn't been in denial, if I'd listened to you—"

She could hear in his tone that he was starting to panic. She couldn't let him fall into that pit, because she wasn't sure she could get him out of it again.

Grabbing his hand, she gripped his fingers. "You've done your best, Gavin. You've always done your best. But right now, we have to focus on finding your daughter. You can talk about what you did or didn't know until you're blue in the face, but not right now. Okay?" She spoke to him almost like she did her students, and to her immense relief, he seemed to respond to her no-nonsense tone. He took in a deep breath, nodding.

"You're right." He laughed a little. "Of course you're right. I just said you were."

"I called Teagan, before I got here. She said that it wasn't my fault that she OD'd." Gavin pushed his fingers through his hair. "All this time, I'd blamed myself, and I was so afraid that Emma would end up sick like her mother."

His voice was so pained that Kat felt near tears once again.

Kat knew that recriminations and regrets weren't going to bring Emma home. An hour passed, and the flurries turned to bigger flakes, dusting their shoulders and hair and the ground around them. She shivered, wishing she'd brought her coat. She'd been so preoccupied she hadn't paid any attention to the weather report.

"When's the last time we had snow around Halloween?"

"Not any time I can remember. It never snows until late December, if even that early." He looked up at the sky. "I'd take this as a bad omen, if I were that kind of a person."

It had started snowing in earnest, collecting on the forest floor. Although there were tons of autumn leaves, there were also spots where the snow made footprints easily visible.

"You should take it as a good omen.." She pointed to tiny footprints made by a squirrel. "See? This is good, at least for now."

She cupped her hands over her mouth. "Emma! Emma, can you hear me? Where are you? Emma!"

They trudged through the woods, and soon with the clouds overhead hiding the sun, they had to turn on the flash-lights provided to them by the police. The beams flashed off of tree trunks and branches, catching on the spots of bright autumnal color still hanging on to some of the branches. It was a strange mix of autumn and winter, with the snow covering the red and orange leaves like this. Kat rather hoped this would be the only snow they got this season, but knowing Missouri weather, they'd have ninety-degree days next week just because.

As the sun began to set, Kat could tell that Gavin was getting more anxious. She couldn't blame him. The snow fell harder, and the temperature continued to drop. They yelled Emma's name over and over again, but all they heard in reply was the echo of other people yelling her name as well.

They were also getting closer to the river, which made

Kat's heart stop as she imagined that Emma had gotten caught in the current. Although the river hadn't been high as of late, it still had nasty currents that could carry you downstream faster than you'd expect. Would Emma have gotten close enough to fall into the water?

When they were close enough to hear the rush of the river, Gavin stopped to drink some water, and he offered Kat the bottle as well. His face was grim, like he was expecting the worst at this point. She had nothing to say now, no words of encouragement. Only prayers, and a spark of hope, that everything would turn out all right.

"Before we keep going, I want to tell you something," he said into the dark night, snowflakes melting on his face. "I didn't just mess up with Emma—I messed everything up with you. I can't tell you how sorry I am. I was an idiot. I hope you can forgive me."

She waited for the three little words she wanted to hear the most, but they never came. *This isn't the time*, she told herself. Despite her disappointment, she also wanted to throw her arms around Gavin. Another part of her wondered if he was just reacting to the emotion of the moment with his sudden apology. Would he have said anything if this hadn't happened?

Kat pushed the negative thoughts away. They weren't going to help them find Emma.

He stepped toward her. "Say something, please."

"We need to find Emma." It was the only thing she could think to say.

His expression shuttered. He nodded tightly and then kept walking.

Please, please, let us find Emma. I'll never ask for anything ever again. Just find her and let me know that she's safe and sound.

As they drew closer and closer to the river, Kat saw a flash of light off to her right. She stilled. Was that a flashlight from one of the search parties? When she saw it flashing multiple times, she had a feeling it wasn't just one of the officers looking for Emma.

She ran toward the illumination, her heart in her throat. Maybe Emma had somehow found a way to signal them, or maybe someone else was signaling to let them know Emma was near. She heard Gavin call after her, but she was too intent on following the light to heed him.

Kat ran and ran, following the light. She sprinted so quickly that she soon could barely hear Gavin calling her own name. She called Emma's name, and then she heard a shout. She ran faster and burst into a clearing some yards from the river.

As she shined her light out into the clearing, her breath caught in her throat when she saw Emma next to a man. As she focused on his figure, she realized it was Silas. He had his arm around Emma. Relief spread through her, but when she saw the fear on Emma's face, she realized that he wasn't there to help the girl.

He hadn't gone to help search for Emma: he'd left to *find* her.

"Silas, let her go," Kat said, her voice barely a whisper. "Let her go--please. You don't want to do this. Can't we talk this out?"

Silas didn't say anything, but instead pulled Emma closer to his side. She whimpered. When Kat approached, Silas smiled, and it sent a shiver down her spine.

"Hi, Kat. I was hoping you'd show up here." His once kind eyes flicked over her, and she couldn't help but feel dirty from his gaze. "And look, I was right. I knew you'd do anything for that son of a bitch and his kid."

She kept her flashlight trained on Silas's face. "Why are you doing this?"

"You can't really think why?" When Emma started to struggle against him, he swore something at her and clamped his arm tighter around her shoulders. Kat was about to run toward them, but he snarled, "Stay where you are."

Her brain couldn't come to grips with what she was seeing. Silas was her friend; he was a *teacher*. He couldn't do something so heinous as threaten to hurt, or kill, a child.

"Silas," said Kat slowly, like he was a wild animal. "This isn't you. You're my friend. You're a good guy."

"I'm well aware that I'm just your *friend*."

Kat realized her misstep. Emma, for her part, was completely still. Kat met her gaze and said, "Don't be afraid, Emma."

"Don't talk to her!" Silas pulled the girl up harder, making Emma cry out. "Say one more word, and she's dead."

Kat had been tip-toeing toward them, but she stopped in her tracks. She put her hands up. "We can talk about this. There's no reason for violence. Do you want to lose everything? Your job, your reputation?" Kat tried to appeal to Silas's logical side—if he even still had one.

He scoffed at her words. "This isn't my fault. It's yours. Can't you see that? I tried to warn you in so many ways. But you wouldn't listen, so I had to take drastic measures. If you'd just listened to me..." His expression turned anguished. "I tried my best. I really did."

Strangely, Kat believed him. In his mind, he'd tried to warn her away from Gavin. The irony was now that the man she should've been warned against was not Gavin Danvers.

"I'm sorry I didn't listen," she lied. "I should have." She inhaled deeply, the pain of her next words splitting her heart open. "We're not together anymore, Gavin and I. It's over. You were right all along. He wasn't the man for me."

Emma's eyes widened, and Kat could see tears forming in her eyes. When she opened her mouth to speak, Kat gave a tiny shake of her head. Emma bit her lip.

"I told you. I told you he'd hurt you." Silas looked crazed now. "You had another option, Kat. You had *me.*"

Right then, Gavin burst through the trees, his breath heaving from his chest. Upon seeing her father, Emma immediately started to struggle, like a cat trying to free itself. Silas raised a hand to strike her.

Kat didn't think: she just ran toward them. She pushed Silas so hard that he lost hold of Emma, almost stumbling to the ground. Emma fell to her hands and knees in the dirt.

"Run, Emma!" Kat screamed as she grappled with Silas.

Gavin shouted something. Kat heard footsteps. And then she felt cold metal against her temple. When she realized what it was, it took all her strength not to scream herself hoarse.

"All those emails, comments," whispered Silas, "but you still went to Gavin fucking Danvers's arms."

Kat couldn't breathe. Suddenly, like a puzzle coming together, she realized that Silas wasn't just a rejected would-be lover: he was also the same person who'd been threatening her for weeks.

"It was you," she breathed. "It was *you.*"

"You finally figured it out. Good job." Silas smiled, but

there was no joy in it. "Took you long enough, though. I always thought you were smarter than that."

"Don't hurt her." Kat looked up to see Gavin with his hands up. "Let her go. You don't want to do this." Gavin took a step forward.

"Don't move," Silas said harshly to Gavin. "Or I'll blow her brains out from here to Sunday."

CHAPTER EIGHTEEN

Gavin heard the yells and ran as fast as his feet could carry him. How had Kat managed to get so far ahead of him? Fear coalesced in his gut that he'd lost her in the woods.

But he soon heard voices and went toward the sounds. Even then, it felt like an eternity before he arrived in the clearing where Kat had stopped. But the sight in front of him instantly arrested him: Silas Fraser holding Emma captive. Gavin was still far enough away that Silas hadn't heard him approach.

Before Gavin could react to the tableau in front of him, Kat launched herself at Silas, screaming at Emma to run for it. A moment later, Gavin caught his daughter in his arms and breathed in her sweet scent.

But he didn't have time to be relieved. Silas now had a gun to Kat's temple. Gavin's heart almost burst out of his chest at the horrifying sight.

Turning to Emma, he said, "I need you to get out of here and get help. Can you do that?" He handed her his flashlight.

"Keep the river on your left and it'll take you straight to people looking for you."

"But what about you?"

"I'll be okay. I love you, baby." He hugged her close and wrapped her fingers around the flashlight. "Now run."

Emma hesitated, but only for a second. She took off, running like the wind. He only hoped she'd find help in time.

"Let her go," Gavin called, announcing his presence.

Silas's head shot up, and he flashed his own light in Gavin's direction. "Oh good. Everyone's here."

"Don't do this." Gavin's voice was a croak, raspy with fear.

Silas scoffed. "I'm tired of everyone doing what you want. I tried my best to get Kat to come to me for help, but she went to you, didn't she? Stupid bitch."

He yanked Kat closer, and Gavin saw her eyes widen. But she didn't cry out. She stood still as a statue, barely trembling, and he only loved her more for it. When had he ever deserved a woman as brave and caring as Kat?

"Take me instead," Gavin insisted. "If you want to hurt someone, hurt me."

"No!" Kat lurched toward him, but Silas only pressed the gun harder to her temple. "Don't do this, Gavin."

Silas rolled his eyes. "As touching as this is, I'm not here for *you*. I'm here for her. I always have been. Tracking you online, too."

Kat looked at Silas with horror, and Gavin realized with a jolt that Silas was the one who'd been terrorizing her for these past weeks.

"Ah, I see you know what I'm talking about. Yes, I was the one sending all of those emails and comments. When I realized Kat was obsessed with you, I thought I could get her to come to me in her terror. I could be a source of comfort. But I didn't reckon she'd be stupid enough to go to you."

Silas turned off the safety on the gun, his finger on the trigger. "So you see, if you take one more step toward us, I'll shoot her. You don't want that, do you?"

"What do you want?" said Gavin.

Silas sneered at Gavin. "I want this woman to apologize for everything she's done. She led me on. She acted like she wanted me but she only wanted you. Some asshole with a crazy ex-wife and an equally crazy kid. What could you give her that I couldn't? I want her on her knees, begging for her life."

He took Kat by the arm and wrenched her down onto the ground, the gun now pointed at her forehead. "Beg, you stupid bitch. Beg for your life, and maybe I'll grant you some measure of mercy."

Kat panted, staring down the barrel of Silas's gun. Gavin watched and tried to find an opening, but Silas wasn't going to let Kat go without a fight. All three knew it.

"Is this about the game?" Gavin took one small step forward as he spoke. He couldn't believe what he was hearing. "You're mad about a computer game?"

Silas rolled his eyes. "The game was just a useful tool. I thought when she started getting harassed, she'd come to me for help." He pressed the gun harder into Kat's forehead. "Why did you have to go to *him*?"

Gavin watched in horror as Silas was about to press the trigger. "If you love her at all, don't do this. Kill me. I'm the one who ruined everything."

Kat trembled even harder, but she didn't say anything.

Silas seemed to consider, then he shrugged. "True, you are

just as much to blame," he reasoned. "So now I'm going to kill her first, and then I'm going to kill you."

Gavin caught Kat's gaze. Her chin was trembling, and tears ran down her cheeks. Gavin felt like his knees were about to collapse under him. The thought of losing Kat was simply unbearable. And to a man like this? A man who'd acted like he was her friend while he'd been threatening her and making her too scared to stay in her own home?

Gavin would go to his grave before he let Silas hurt the woman he loved.

"Baby," he said to Kat, taking in her beautiful face. "I'm sorry for everything. I love you. I should've told you sooner, but I'll do everything I can to make it up to you."

Silas cried out. "Shut up! Shut the fuck up! You don't get to talk to her like that!"

"Silas, you know you don't want to do this." Tears dripped down Kat's face. "If you ever cared about me, you'll let me go. I won't even press charges. You can just go."

Silas's hand holding the gun began to tremble. "I don't believe you."

"When have I ever given you a reason not to trust me?"

He let out a sharp laugh. "The day you started fucking *this* man!" In a fit of rage, he pistol-whipped Kat, and she collapsed to the ground.

Gavin let out a roar. He rushed at Silas, taking him straight to the ground with a grunt. Gavin heard distant shouting, but it barely registered. All his focus was on the gun in Silas's hands.

"Run!" he yelled to Kat. "Go find Emma and get help!"

He didn't wait for Kat to respond. He couldn't let Silas use that gun, no matter what happened. The two men grappled for the weapon as they rolled on the ground, stuck in a life and death struggle. A rock dug into Gavin's knee, causing a sharp pain to run up his leg. Silas was now on his back. Gavin got in two punches to the man's face and then hit him so hard on his wrist that Silas finally dropped the gun. Before Gavin could grab it, though, Silas somehow managed to kick Gavin in the stomach so hard that the wind was knocked out of him.

Gavin bent over in half, gasping for breath. Silas, though, wasn't done yet, and he rose and kicked Gavin in the ribs. Gavin curled in on himself just as he heard a man shout, "Drop your weapons!"

But the only thing on Gavin's mind was survival. He rolled away from Silas's kicks and got to his feet, panting. Silas's face was bloodied, and just as Gavin was about to take him down again, the man ran toward the gun that he'd dropped. Gavin sprinted after him. He crashed into Silas from the side right as Silas lifted up the gun, and everything seemed to slow down when the sound of the gun firing went off through the clearing.

A woman screamed. Time seemed to stop. Gavin found himself lying on the ground, warmth spreading next to him. He looked to his side, and Silas lay there, gasping for breath.

"Gavin, Gavin!" Kat was kneeling beside him. "Can you hear me? Gavin!"

He had the strangest urge to close his eyes, but he couldn't look away from Kat. He reached up to touch her face; he felt wetness on her cheeks. "I love you, Kat," he breathed.

"I know. I've always known. You stupid, moronic, brave idiot." She was sobbing now.

Her hands were also searching his body, and he didn't understand why she was doing this now and here of all places.

He cried out when she pressed hard against his side. His eyelids fluttered closed.

He'd been shot. He'd been *shot.* His mind was trying to accept this fact, but it seemed too crazy. Even as Kat pressed harder against the wound, the pain started to fade.

Kat gasped out, "If you die on me, Gavin Danvers, I will find your ghost and haunt you for eternity. Do you hear me?" Kat's voice was ragged, and he wanted to tell her there was no way he was leaving her, but his voice didn't seem to work anymore.

After that, more people arrived, and lights flashed, and there were shouts, and his eyelids became so heavy that he couldn't keep them open anymore. Darkness embraced him.

CHAPTER NINETEEN

When Gavin awoke, the first thing he noticed was the astringent scent of his surroundings. He didn't understand why the woods would smell like that, but when he opened his eyes, he slowly realized he was no longer in the woods. He was in the hospital. The hospital? Why was he in the hospital?

"You're awake." Kat touched his arm, her eyes shining as she looked down at him. "Jesus Christ, Gavin."

He saw that she was crying, and he reached up to wipe the tears away. "What happened?" His voice was croaky.

"You were shot, but the bullet just grazed you. You bled quite a bit, though." She sniffled. "Scared me half to death, too."

In a rush, it all came back to him: the woods, Kat, Silas, Emma. *Emma.* He lurched upward, but groaned as his wound smarted. "Emma? Where is she? Is she all right?"

Kat grabbed his hands to still him. "She's okay. She found help, just like you told her to. She was so brave. They arrested Silas. It's over."

"How did he get Emma? How did this even happen?"

Kat sighed. "Apparently Silas was planning to hurt me, but when he stumbled upon Emma hiding in the supply closet, he decided she'd be bait. He wanted to use her to get to me, and to you. He left me a note telling me to come alone to the woods, but I didn't see it until after it was all over." She gave a wry, sad smile. "It wasn't a good plan, and for that, I'm grateful."

"Where's Emma?" He needed to see his daughter, to make sure she really was okay. His eyes stung, remembering how Silas had kept her captive. He remembered the gun Silas had pointed at Kat, and the fear flooded through him, making him tremble.

"She just went to get something to eat. Everyone's here— your entire family. They're looking after her. Teagan is trying to get here, too."

Gavin breathed out a sigh of relief, then winced. Apparently, painkillers didn't get rid of all of the pain.

"What happened after I was shot?" he asked, taking Kat's hand.

Her lower lip trembled. "You don't remember? The EMTs and police had to carry you out of the woods on a stretcher."

"No, I don't remember anything." He rubbed his temples. "I remember fighting with Silas, I remember telling Emma to run…"

"They raced you into the hospital to stabilize you, but then they had to medflight you to Columbia for surgery."

Gavin finally took in his surroundings, realizing that this hospital room was too fancy to be the local one. "How long have I been asleep?"

"For two days. Gavin, they weren't sure you'd pull

through." Kat's eyes glimmered with unshed tears. "The bullet came within a quarter inch of an major artery. Any closer, and you would've bled out."

Strangely, he didn't feel afraid when he heard those words —that he'd nearly died just a few days ago. All Gavin could feel was an immense tiredness, and the need to see his daughter's face. But most of all, he hated to see Kat crying. It broke his heart as much as the bullet had broken his body.

"But I'm here, aren't I? I survived." He squeezed Kat's hand. "Lie down next to me."

She sniffled. "What?"

"I want to feel you. I've missed you."

"You've been high as a kite for two days." She smiled slightly and snuggled up next to him in the hospital bed. It was a tight fit, and if he weren't full of painkillers, he might find it uncomfortable. But then he smelled Kat's sweet scent, felt her hair brush his chin, and he didn't care one bit.

His IV started beeping. And beeping. And beeping. Kat let out an annoyed huff and moved his arm. The beeping continued. She moved his arm a second time. Finally by the third try, the IV stopped complaining.

"What was that?" said Gavin.

"When there's a kink in the line, it gets mad. You kept moving your arm in your sleep and making it beep. The nurses kept having to come into your room and get it to stop."

He chuckled. "You mean I'm a pain in the ass even when unconscious?"

"Pretty much." Kat sighed, laying her head on his shoulder. "But it meant that you were still alive, though. I'd listen to that stupid thing beep for eternity if it meant you were still here."

He kissed the top of her head, his fingers brushing against

her temple. The touch made her wince. He looked more closely to see that she had a bruise that size of a small plum.

"Baby, what the hell? Did he hurt you?" Rage filled Gavin.

She looked up at him in confusion. "You don't remember? He hit me with his gun."

"Jesus Christ. I'll kill him. For everything, I'll fucking kill that son of a bitch."

"Not if I don't kill him first."

Gavin grunted. "Never took you for blood-thirsty."

"He kidnapped Emma, threatened to kill her. He almost killed *you.* So yeah, I'm just as angry with him as you are." Kat sighed again. "But I'm also angry with myself."

"What? Why?"

"I should've known Silas was no good. There were so many red flags, but I just attributed it to him being an odd guy. I never thought he was capable of something like this, but if I hadn't been so naïve…"

"Kat, look at me."

Kat hesitated, but Gavin lifted her chin.

"Do not, under any circumstance, blame yourself. The only person whose fault this is is Silas. No one else. He made the choice to terrorize you and then to keep acting like he was your friend. He let himself get taken over by jealousy. He chose to do everything. You aren't to blame."

"I'm just saying if I'd been less naïve, I could've prevented all of this." Tears ran down Kat's face. "The moment you were shot, I knew I could never forgive myself if you died. You fought to protect me from a man who I should've known was bad news since the beginning." Her voice cracked. "I should've known, I should've known."

Gavin shushed her, rubbing his chin against her hair as

she cried. His brain was mush from the painkillers, and he struggled to convince her not to feel guilty. All he could tell her, over and over again, was that she shouldn't blame herself. But he knew Kat: she had a good heart, and she took it hard when things happened that were out of her control.

Hell, he was the same, wasn't he? He'd blamed himself for Teagan's overdose. He'd blamed himself for letting Kat go out of sheer fear.

If anyone was to blame, it was him, for not protecting his family like he should have.

"Please don't cry," he begged. "You'll really kill me if you don't stop. I'm begging you."

She let a little laugh. "I had no idea tears could get you to do whatever I wanted."

"Now you know: just cry and I'm putty in your hands."

He and Kat lay quietly for a bit, and Gavin simply listened to her breathing. He was about to fall asleep when the door to his room opened, and there was Emma. Her face lit up when she saw that Gavin was awake.

"Dad!" She ran toward him and clambered up onto the bed right as Kat got down.

He didn't care that Emma jostled his wound; he didn't care that his IV started beeping as he wrapped her in his arms. He held her tight, breathing in her sweet scent, reveling in the feeling of her warmth and vitality.

"Emma, sweetheart," he said in a rasp. "God, it's good to see you."

"You're going to be okay?" Her lower lip trembled.

"I'm not going anywhere." He hugged her again before she curled against his side.

"I was so scared." Emma's face was pale. "I wasn't sure you'd find me in time."

"I'll always find you. Remember that," replied Gavin.

Emma nodded, burying her face against his shoulder. Kat rubbed Emma's back.

"She's been so brave through all of this," said Kat in wonder. "Haven't you, Emma?"

Emma just shrugged. "What else was I supposed to do?"

Gavin knew that his daughter was simply too young to process what had happened to her. He thought of how scared she must've been, and it tore him up inside. His only wish was that his entire family could heal from this, because Silas didn't deserve to have the satisfaction.

"Aunt Joy let me watch *Frozen* every day," said Emma. "She even let me watch it when I kept having bad dreams."

Despite the seriousness of the conversation, Gavin smiled because he knew that Emma rewatching *Frozen* over and over would've been a huge sacrifice for Adam, since his brother couldn't stand musicals. To have "Let It Go" playing at all hours of the day and night? Gavin owed his brother—big time.

"What else did you do while I was asleep?" said Gavin.

Emma shrugged. "Nothing, really."

Kat caught his gaze, and he knew that that answer was loaded with meaning. Gavin wanted to ask his daughter about her bad dreams; he wanted to reassure her that she'd never go through something like this again. The only reason he wasn't breaking down completely was because his brain was foggy. Once he got out of the hospital and was no longer on painkillers, he knew a reckoning would be coming.

"I'm just glad you're safe," said Gavin, holding Emma close

and enclosing Kat's hand with his. "Both of you. My girls. My brave, beautiful girls."

"Do you think I was as brave as Kat?" said Emma.

"You were both brave. Extremely brave. I'm proud of you both."

A memory slowly formed in his brain. The encounter with Silas was patchy at best, but talking about it now seemed to bring it into clearer focus. Bits and pieces tugged at his memory, including one piece that made his breath catch in his throat.

He stroked Emma's hair with a trembling hand as he looked up at Kat, shaking his head. " I can't believe you threw yourself at Silas." He clutched at her hand. "That was so stupid, Kat."

She laughed a little. "Maybe, but it worked. I'm okay. Just a little bruised up, but better than you." She arched an eyebrow, and he knew she was trying to keep things light for Emma. "I'm not the one who got shot."

He sighed, and he took her hand to kiss the back of it. "I love you, Kat," he said. "I'm sorry I was such a coward. I don't deserve you, you know."

"I know that." At his expression, she grinned. "I love you, too, you stubborn man." She leaned toward him and they kissed, but Emma made a disgruntled noise, which caused them to part and laugh.

"I am sitting right here," Emma said pertly. But then she looked up at Kat and asked, "Are you going to be my stepmom?"

Kat raised an eyebrow. "Maybe. Your dad hasn't asked me, though."

"Ladies, ladies. Let a guy recover first before we start

talking about weddings." But the thought of Kat becoming his wife, walking down the aisle toward him, wearing a beautiful white gown? It didn't make him want to turn tail and run. He only wanted to embrace it and see what the future would bring them.

The rest of the Danvers clan came in, with everyone surrounding Gavin and asking him how he was feeling, what he remembered, and every other question under the sun. Kat had filled them in as much as she could, but everyone wanted to talk to Gavin. He tried his best, but after about an hour of questions, he looked so exhausted that Kat shooed everyone out.

The nurse came in and gave him another dose of morphine. Gavin tried to fight the sleep that wanted to claim him, but his eyelids were so heavy that he wouldn't last long.

"Emma, can you tell me what happened?"

Emma plucked at the sheets, avoiding his gaze. He jostled her a little. "Tell me," he breathed.

"I got scared," she mumbled.

When she didn't seem like she'd continue, Kat rubbed her back. "You can talk to us, Emma."

"I had a dream the night before, that Mom was going to die. I tried to stop thinking about it. I did. But it got so bad that I went to the closet, like before. That's when Mr. Fraser found me." She looked up at Gavin with wide eyes. "He took me into the woods, but I tried hard to stop him. I really did."

Gavin sighed. Sleep was claiming him, but he said in a slurred voice, "I'm sorry, Emma. I'm sorry you were scared and that you felt like you had to run away. I'm sorry that man took you, and I promise you, I will never let that happen again. When you're ready, though, we're going to have you talk to some people to help you not be so scared anymore."

Emma burrowed against him. "I don't like talking to people."

"I know, but I'm going to talk to some people, too. I promise. We'll do it together." He yawned, and he took Emma's hand just as sleep finally took hold of him and wouldn't let go.

Two months after what was eventually termed The Incident, everything seemed to return to normal. Mostly normal, at any rate, Kat reflected with a wry smile. Gavin had told her in no uncertain terms that there was no way she was going to get away from him again, and she'd moved in with him the day he'd returned home from the hospital. And neither of them had looked back.

Silas awaited his trial, sitting in jail for the foreseeable future. The judge had denied him bail since he would still be a real threat to Kat, Gavin and Emma. Silas had tried contacting Kat to apologize, but she'd refused all contact. He'd told the judge that he'd done everything because he loved her. She didn't understand it, but she was glad he couldn't hurt anyone else.

The past two months had been ones of healing. Gavin had mostly healed from his bullet wound, although he still had pain in his side if he worked himself too hard. More than once, Kat had had to convince him to rest. It didn't help that he'd been unable to work at River's Bend and had to instead use his savings to pay for living expenses until he got back onto his feet. He'd briefly mentioned that his family had said they would assist him, but Gavin had too much pride for that, the stubborn man.

Gavin had also found a child therapist for Emma, along with one for himself as well. Emma's anxiety had gotten worse in the beginning, and she'd suffered from nightmares more than once when Kat had stayed the night with Gavin. Gavin had been beside himself with guilt. Kat had encouraged him to seek therapy for not just his daughter, but for himself.

"If we're all going to therapy, you should go, too," he'd said wryly. "You can't tell me this entire thing didn't affect you, either."

Kat had tried to keep her fears to herself, the anxiety that kept her awake the nights she spent at her grandmother's house. She'd told herself that with Silas behind bars, she had nothing to fear. But that didn't stop her from looking over her shoulder when she heard a strange noise, or seeing the woods behind the school and remembering.

So she'd found a therapist, too, and all of them began to heal from the wounds inflicted that cold October night. Even as the physical wounds healed, the emotional wounds would take much longer.

But Kat had Gavin and Emma's love, and she loved them both with her entire heart. They healed each other with every moment they spent together. Kat could see a future that was bright and hopeful, not terrifying and lonely.

A few days before Christmas, Kat spent most of her time at Gavin's. The apartment could barely hold three people, but it was cozy on cold winter days.

Emma was asleep already. Kat was curled up next to

Gavin, a mug of hot cider warming her hands. Gavin was rubbing her neck and giving her occasional forehead kisses. Christmas music played softly in the background. The only thing they lacked was a fire. Too bad Gavin's little apartment didn't have a fireplace, she thought drowsily.

"You're so beautiful," said Gavin, gazing down at her. "You know that, right?"

"Considering you say it all the time…" She smiled and touched his face. "You're pretty too, you know."

To her amusement, he looked embarrassed. "I'm hardly *pretty*."

"You're very pretty." He made a sound, and she laughed. "You're also handsome, and so manly that you can rip logs apart with your bare hands. You drip testosterone with every step you take. I'm pretty much pregnant just from sitting next to you."

That made him growl. "You're damn right I am."

Kat had the forethought to set her mug of cider down right before Gavin tumbled her back onto the couch, caging her in with his arms and legs. She laughed. Despite the prison of his embrace, she didn't want to be anywhere else. There was no one she felt safer with than with Gavin Danvers.

"Take back what you said," he said before kissing her jaw.

"That you can split logs with your bare hands?"

"No, that I'm pretty."

She snorted. "Are you seriously still harping about that." She let out a surprised moan when his hands brushed her upraised nipple.

"If you don't, I'm going to punish you. All night long."

She raked her fingers through his dark hair. "Sounds terrible. Maybe I should call the police."

"Our neighbors probably will once they hear you screaming."

She couldn't help but laugh at that pronouncement, which only gave Gavin more reason to show her how determined he was. He kissed her, claiming her mouth, his hands skating across her body. He knew exactly how to touch her, and how to draw out her desire until she trembled for him.

He pushed her sweater up and cupped her breast through the lace material of her bra. "Somebody is turned on," he said with a low laugh.

"It's just cold."

"What a bad liar you are." He tweaked her nipple at the same time he sucked on the side of her neck. She'd never understood the appeal of hickeys—until Gavin had given her one. Now she enjoyed them a little too much for an adult woman.

He whispered words against her ear, making her blush and her body heat up further. When he pushed her jeans down and his fingers delved below the elastic of her panties, she could've cried with joy. But he only danced his hand across her sex. When she tried to get him to touch her where she needed him most, he just chuckled, the jerk.

He played and petted her, giving her only a taste of what she wanted. Frustrated, she cupped his hardened length and squeezed. Gavin hissed in a breath, his eyes turning dark.

"You're playing with fire," he rasped.

"Well, I'll be cliché and say that I want to get burned."

Gavin kissed her hard. They undulated their bodies against each other, needing that friction but not quite getting it. Soon they were tearing off their clothes, their things flying in every which way.

Gavin pulled Kat on top of him, his cock pressing against her. He tugged on her nipples.

"Perfect," was all he said.

Kat was already wet and open, and she slid onto his cock with a relieved breath. Gavin bucked under her. Both of them were already close to the edge. Leaning over him, Kat began to grind slowly, loving the way his pelvis brushed her clit while his cock filled her completely.

"I love you," she said, digging her fingers into his shoulder.

"I love you." He gripped her hair. "So much."

Kat closed her eyes, feeling the orgasm creeping into her. And then it burst inside of her. She buried her face against Gavin's shoulder to stifle the sound. When she began to shake, he grunted, his own release pushing through him.

He kissed her until her lips felt bruised, his cock still inside of her. God, she loved this man. She'd never known love like this, and she was so grateful that they'd managed to find each other in this crazy world.

Gavin pulled a blanket of them both as Kat snuggled into him. After some minutes of silence, he said, "What are you thinking about?"

"I'm thinking about how pretty you look when you tell me that you love me."

Gavin snorted, and Kat laughed, and he then proceeded to show Kat exactly how a pretty man like him could love her.

Now, sitting with Joy at her wedding on Christmas Eve, Kat reflected that she'd never been happier than she had been these past two months. The Incident aside, she'd fallen in love with Gavin Danvers even more than she had before, if that was possible. He'd done everything in his power to make up for turning her away, and she'd let him. She smiled, thinking of how he'd made things up to her just this morning.

"What are you smiling about?" Joy looked at her in the mirror, where she was putting the finishing touches on her makeup. Unsurprisingly, she wore a dress that wasn't remotely traditional: instead of white, she wore a creamy pink gown with flowers trailing down the back, like a waterfall of petals. It brought out the peachy creaminess of her skin, and Kat rather thought she looked like a queen wearing it. She didn't wear any jewelry except the engagement ring on her finger, which would soon have a wedding band added to it.

"I'm just so happy to finally see you and Adam get married and stop living in sin," Kat quipped.

Joy rolled her eyes. "Takes one to know one. Besides, there was no way I was marrying Adam without planning the wedding I wanted. He would've run to the courthouse if I'd said yes."

Kat smiled. "Gavin said the same thing to me."

"Did he ask you?" Joy whirled to face her. "Kat Williamson, don't play with me! Are you engaged?"

She could only nod, and Joy squealed with delight. But seeing that her left hand was bare, Joy made a face.

Kat couldn't help but laugh. "He kind of asked me without planning the rest of it. But don't worry, I'm getting the biggest ring out of him I can."

"Good. You deserve it." Joy stood up and hugged her, and Kat suddenly fought tears. "I'm so glad you're part of the family now, Kat."

So was Kat. Gavin hadn't been the only one to overcome

his fears: Kat had as well. She'd realized she'd kept herself alone to avoid getting hurt, but Gavin had shown her that, for love, the risk was always worth it.

The door opened, and Grace entered. She wore the silvery bridesmaid dress that Kat also wore, and her blonde hair was piled on top of her head. She looked absolutely radiant, and Kat had to wonder if Grace Danvers had a secret of her own.

"Adam wanted me to ask if you were ready," Grace asked.

Joy raised an eyebrow. "And you can ask him if *he's* ready." Then she smiled. "I'm as ready as I'll ever be."

Grace practically bounced on her toes, and Kat eyed her. Was she touching her abdomen more often than usual, or was she imagining things? She bit her lip to keep from smiling too obviously as she asked, "Does Jaime know?"

Grace's head whipped toward her, her fingers pressing against her stomach. When Joy noticed the gesture, she gasped. "Grace Danvers!" Joy breathed. "Tell me right now what's going on!"

Grace blushed and sat down beside them, and they huddled together as a group. "I just found out this past week. I told Jaime last night." If it was possible, she blushed harder. "I'm pregnant."

The sound they all made together was enough to wake the dead. Joy hugged Grace so hard that she rumpled her gown, and Grace's hair was in danger of falling from its pins. Kat hugged her as well.

"Congratulations. How did Jaime take it?" Kat asked.

"He's still kind of in a daze. But then this morning he was so happy that he couldn't stop kissing me." Grace bit back a smile. "That's why we were late."

Joy smacked her on the arm. "For shame! But I'm so happy for you two. You'll make the best parents."

"What about you?" Grace poked Joy in the arm. "Are you guys working on any project? Not that I'm dying to know what either of you are doing with my brothers, but tit for tat and all that."

Joy shrugged, but it was an elusive gesture. "We'll see, won't we?"

Kat looked at the time. "Joy, if we don't leave now, you'll be late to your own wedding."

The ceremony went off without a hitch, the bride looking gorgeous and the groom looking like he couldn't believe how lucky he was. Kat gazed at Gavin as they stood up for Adam and Joy, and he mouthed the words *I love you* at her more than once.

Unlike the unseasonal snow they'd gotten around Halloween, this Christmas Eve was the warmest they'd had in decades. Although they'd planned to have the reception inside the vineyard's main building, they were able to set up tents outside with heaters running.

Kat and Gavin stopped to speak with Officer Haldon, who'd been so helpful during and after The Incident. Kat had quickly discovered that Matt Haldon was wise beyond his years, and he'd gone above and beyond the call of duty. He'd stopped by Gavin's apartment to ask how everyone was doing. Most of all, he'd been instrumental in convincing the judge not to allow Silas to have the chance to post bail.

"So glad you could come," said Gavin, giving Matt a pat on the shoulder.

Matt looked a little embarrassed. "Am I allowed to say that weddings make me feel awkward?"

"You and every other man," replied Gavin.

Kat just rolled her eyes at her boyfriend. "You're such a liar. You were teary-eyed the entire ceremony."

"That was allergies."

Matt gave them both an amused look. "Well, I appreciate the invitation anyway. I'm glad to see your family is doing well."

Gavin's expression turned serious. "You know I can't thank you enough for all of your help."

"You've said it a few times. It's my job. Don't even worry about it."

Matt said goodbye, heading toward the wine bar. Kat had heard that Matt had a girlfriend, but he hadn't brought a plus one to the wedding.

"What's that look?" said Gavin with suspicion.

"Just thinking."

"About?"

"How a great guy like Matt could be single, that's all."

Gavin snorted. "Don't turn matchmaker, Kat. I doubt Matt would thank you for it."

Kat didn't reply, only because she didn't have anyone in mind for Matt. But if she met a great woman who'd be interested in dating a great guy… Well, wasn't it her civic duty to help things along?

"I'm just so happy with you that I want everyone else to be happy, too," she said as Gavin led her out to the dance floor.

He couldn't help but smile at that. "Okay, I'll give you that." He kissed her forehead.

Kat tilted her head back to look into his eyes. "I love you," she said.

"I know." When she pinched him, he added, "I love you,

too. I adore you, actually, and I'm going to buy you the most amazing engagement ring to show off."

She smiled. "I don't need a huge ring, but I won't say no, either." She kissed him, and then they danced together, swaying to the music.

Later, Emma cut in, and Gavin danced with his daughter. Emma was already making strides, and her episodes had grown less frequent since she—and Gavin—had started seeing a therapist. Emma had been diagnosed with an anxiety disorder, but Gavin hadn't taken it as hard as he might have months earlier. He knew that Emma wasn't Teagan, and that he couldn't blame himself for Teagan's struggles, either.

After Gavin had gotten out of the hospital, Teagan had arrived, in a frenzy and desperate to see her daughter. She hugged Emma until the girl couldn't breathe, and Kat finally had the opportunity to meet the woman she'd been so curious about. Teagan was a slight thing, all blonde and wispy, but her eyes revealed how much she'd gone through. When Teagan had hugged her, thanking her for helping her daughter, Kat had hugged her back and hoped with everything inside of her that Teagan found her own happiness, too.

Gavin told her later that he and Teagan had had a much-needed talk. After they'd discussed everything that had happened between them, Teagan had apparently looked him straight in the eye and said, "It wasn't your fault. It wasn't anyone's fault." She'd then squeezed his hands. "You couldn't save me, Gavin, but that doesn't mean you failed. It just means that the illness was stronger than any of us. But I'm getting through it. Every day I'm better. And soon I'll be able to be the mother Emma deserves."

As Kat watched Gavin and Emma now, her heart warmed.

Her new family meant everything to her. How had she gotten so lucky?

The pair of them came up to her and grabbed her, hauling her onto the dance floor as she laughed. They danced together, happiness and love flowing through them, and Kat knew without a shadow of a doubt that they'd all live happily ever after.

HOLD ME CLOSE

A HERON'S LANDING NOVELLA

After a messy break-up, police officer Matthew Haldon is fine living in his cabin out in the woods all by himself. He has his dogs to keep him company and his job to keep him busy.

He never expects to find love again, especially not with the woman he finds stranded on the side of the road during a blizzard. When Matt realizes that Holly Cook has nowhere to go, he invites her to stay at his cabin for the night.

Holly is dangerous, though: with her fiery red hair and her bubbly personality, she tempts Matt like no woman ever has. As the snowstorm rages outside, Matt and Holly share a night that neither will forget.

Yet Holly's past isn't about to let her go—and now, neither is Matt.

AUTHOR'S NOTE

Dear Readers,

Before you begin Matt and Holly's story, please know that *Hold Me Close* was previously published under the title *Adore Me Ardently*. This second edition has been lightly edited and changed to better fit the overall feel of the rest of my catalogue.

All my best,
Iris

CHAPTER ONE

When Officer Matthew Haldon saw the flash of orange-red in his rearview mirror, he first thought it was a fox running about in this blizzard. When he peered more closely, he realized it wasn't a fox: it was a person. A person most decidedly stranded in a ditch on the side of the road.

Matt had been on the police force for five years now, four of those here in the tiny Missouri town of Heron's Landing. At the moment, he wanted to get home safely, put his feet up, and maybe drink some spiked cider. Sighing, he knew that wasn't going to be happening any time soon. He slowly did a U-turn, the snow falling so hard that you couldn't see more than foot in front of you. Living in a place like Heron's Landing made driving in the snow both a blessing and a curse: a blessing, because you were often alone on the road; a curse, because you were often alone on the road.

After what seemed like an hour, he finally got to the car and the person trying to dig themselves out. He turned on his lights so no poor soul would run into him, and he tromped into the ditch.

"Hello!" he called out. "Are you all right?"

A head popped up from the other side, with that flash of orange-red again. Then, to his astonishment, the person turned out to be a woman, and not only a woman, but a gorgeous, red-haired woman who also wasn't wearing a coat.

So not only was she beautiful, she was crazy.

"Ma'am, do you have a coat? You'll freeze to death."

The woman waded through the snow, laughing. "I forgot my coat! Can you believe that? I packed everything but my coat." She brushed snow off of her long-sleeved t-shirt and shrugged. "I'm more concerned about my flat tire, though."

Matt took in the woman, his chest constricting despite himself. She was rosy-cheeked, with the fullest lips he'd ever seen. She didn't seem the least bit dismayed regarding her situation.

So, yes, a high probability she was crazy.

"Let me drive you somewhere," he offered. "It's snowing too hard to put on a spare. Do you live around here?" Matt knew everyone in Heron's Landing, and this woman was definitely not someone he'd ever seen before.

The woman's initial good cheer faded. She bit her lip. "I was on my way to Kansas City. I don't know anyone around here. Is there a hotel or something close by?"

Matt considered. He could drive back to town—some ten miles, in a blizzard—or he could be a good Samaritan and let this woman stay with him in his house that was only a mile away.

You just want to spend more time with her, his mind reasoned, but he told his mind to shut up.

"The closest hotel is ten miles from here." The woman's shoulders slumped, and without considering it further, he added, "But you're welcome to stay with me. Until the snow stops. Then we can get a tow truck out here to get your car and get you back on the road."

The woman considered, her eyes narrowed. She walked toward him. "How do I know you aren't some serial killer?"

He raised his eyebrows. "I'm a police officer, ma'am."

"That doesn't matter. You could be faking being an officer just to lure unsuspecting women to your house."

"In a blizzard? That seems like a lot of work to me."

She blinked away the snowflakes caught on her lashes, and then her face broke into a smile that hit Matt right in the gut.

"Okay, I'll take your offer." She thrust out a hand, and he took it. "I'm Holly, by the way. You are?"

"Matt. Officer Matt Haldon."

"Great. Now if you could just help me get my suitcase out from underneath all of this crap…"

After wrestling with more "crap" than he could've thought could be stuffed into one woman's trunk, Matt drove Holly back to his place. She shivered, and he turned up the heat until he was sweating underneath his heavy coat. But she sighed in pleasure, which went straight to his groin.

Down, boy. She's your guest. Nothing more.

Matt had broken up with his girlfriend over a year ago, and he hadn't dated much since. It didn't help that there was a dearth of eligible women here in Heron's Landing. He wasn't much for hook-ups, either, so he'd remained celibate for the past twelve months.

That celibacy came to bite him in the ass right now. He'd taken one look at Holly and his body had practically jumped at her. If he weren't so annoyed with himself, he'd laugh at how predictable he was.

Holly rubbed her arms.

"Are you still cold?" he asked.

"I'm okay. I still can't believe I forgot my coat. Then again, I'm not used to winters like this."

"Where are you from?"

She hesitated, and he wondered what she was running from. A bad relationship? Money troubles?

Finally, she replied, "Louisiana. We don't get much snow down there."

Now that he listened more closely, her accent had a slight Southern twang to it, although it was subtle. She must've lived there only for a short time, as she sounded more Midwestern overall.

"So you decided to go on a road trip three days before Christmas but forgot to bring a coat?"

She nodded. "It was…sudden. I was distracted."

"I guess you aren't driving home for Christmas dinner?"

"Not exactly."

They fell silent. Matt turned on the radio, and Christmas music filled the patrol car. His own family lived in Illinois, and his current work schedule hadn't allowed him to go home. Thus, he was spending Christmas alone. He'd told himself he didn't care, but if he were being honest, he was rather depressed about it. It was the first Christmas without Melanie, the first time they wouldn't cook dinner together and open presents underneath the tree.

After driving very slowly through the blinding snow, Matt turned down the lane to get to his house, a two-story cabin that he'd built three years ago with Melanie in mind. Now it just reminded him of his ex-girlfriend with every curtain, every piece of furniture. When they'd broken up, Melanie had told him that she didn't want to live in this hell hole anymore —her words, not his.

I can't do this anymore, she'd said, like he'd forced her to live with him and love him. *I'm sorry, but I can't.*

He shook off the memories as he helped Holly with her luggage. Opening the door, he flipped on the hall light to reveal two excited dogs barking and dancing excitedly in front of them.

Matt crouched in front of the canines. "This is Arya, and this is Sansa."

The two mutts—he thought they were part lab, part setter, and part who knew what—wagged their tails so hard they were in danger of falling over.

Holly leaned down to pet Arya, who snuffled. "*Game of Thrones* fan?"

"Yeah. At least, I was. The names were my ex's idea."

At the mention of Melanie, they both fell silent, and Matt silently cursed himself. *Way to go. How about you share all of your dirty laundry before she even sits down?*

"I think I'm going to take a shower to warm up," Holly said.

Matt jumped up, guilt assailing him. Here she was, freezing and tired, and he was talking about his ex-girlfriend. "Of course. Let me show you to your room. Arya, Sansa, go lie down."

After showing Holly to her room and the adjoining bathroom, Matt went downstairs to stare inside his fridge. Beer, shredded cheese, two eggs, and an almost empty half-gallon of milk. He went to the pantry, and he found a bag of rice that was probably older than this house and not much else. Thinking back, he couldn't remember the last time he'd gone grocery shopping. He'd gotten take-out or gone to the one bar in Heron's Landing as opposed to cooking at home for the most part since he'd broken up with Melanie, and now he cursed himself for being such a lazy bachelor. He couldn't very well feed Holly old rice and beer, now could he?

All thoughts of food fled when Holly came downstairs, her hair wrapped in a towel and wearing some fancy robe over what he assumed was a nightgown. She looked fresh and clean, her cheeks scrubbed until they were rosy, and she smelled like flowers.

She glanced down at her attire and smiled at his expression. "I really hate wearing real clothes around the house," she explained. "And we're snowed in, so why keep my jeans on? Plus, I hate wearing a bra." She scrunched her nose—her adorable, pert little nose—and Matt almost dropped the beer he'd just grabbed from the fridge.

He did not need to think about Holly not wearing a bra. Did she want to kill him? She was going to kill him.

He scrabbled around in the drawer for a bottle opener, trying to banish the thought of what Holly looked like without a bra on—or anything at all.

After finally finding the opener and taking a slug of beer, he said apologetically, "I don't have much food."

She opened his fridge and then laughed. "Do you even eat?" She shook a bag of what he thought was maybe broccoli at him. "Look at this! You're such a guy."

"I'm not much for cooking, I guess."

"I can see that." She pulled out cheese, butter, and then snagged the loaf of bread from the counter. "Where's your skillet? Oh, and do you have mayo? Wait, of course you do. Mmm, let me cut some of these veggies up, and I'll make us some grilled cheeses you'll never forget."

Holly shooed him from the kitchen, rather like a wife would, and Matt sat down in the living room, hearing her hum to herself as she cooked. He stared at the snow falling outside, his heart beating fast, and he wondered if this was all a dream. How had he ended up with this gorgeous, lovely woman in his house? And for the night?

He drank his beer, tipping it back until he'd finished it in only a few gulps.

"Here we go." Holly stepped into the living room, Sansa and Arya right next to her, and placed the plates on the table in front of the couch. "Eat up. I'm starving."

Matt dug into the cheesy goodness, practically moaning at how she'd managed to make the cheese both crispy and gooey. He hadn't had a grilled cheese since he was a kid.

"This is amazing." He glanced at the sandwich again. "I didn't even know I had red onion in the fridge. Wait, is this Gouda? How the hell did you find Gouda around here?"

"I have special powers. What do you eat every night, though, pizza? Wings?"

He shrugged. "Sometimes pizza and wings."

"Well then, aren't you glad I showed up to get your butt in gear." She took a big bite of sandwich and made a little sound in the back of her throat, which only drove Matt even crazier.

When they'd finished eating, and Matt had given a bite each to the dogs who now rested at their feet, he asked, "Why were you headed to Kansas City?"

Holly seemed to close in on herself, and he regretted the question immediately. She shrugged, taking off the towel and letting her red hair fall down to her shoulders. She began to braid it with absentminded strokes.

"I just needed to get away, that's all," she finally said.

"I get that. Sometimes this town gets to be too much, even though it's not even 300 people. My family lives in Illinois, but I couldn't get there this year. So it's just me and the dogs for Christmas."

He knew he was rambling, but it was better than feeling Holly's silence and dismay. He watched as she braided her hair, her face contemplative. When she realized she didn't have something to tie off the braid, she flung it over her shoulder and turned to him.

"Let's not talk about me. What about you?" She waited in expectation.

About him? He was nobody. He was a cop in a small town doing his job. But she was waiting, so he cleared his throat and replied, "I've been a cop for five years. I grew up in Illinois. I hate peas."

She frowned. "Matt. Come on, tell me..." She thought a moment. "Tell me what you wanted to be when you grew up."

That was easy. "A police officer."

"Seriously? Okay, then, where all have you traveled?"

"Illinois, Missouri, Kansas. I went to Iowa once for a basketball tournament in high school. That's it." He couldn't help but smile at her expression. "I'm a boring person, I'm afraid."

"Nobody's boring. You just say that. For instance, my grandma never traveled outside of her town until she was thirty, but she was the most fascinating person I've ever met.

She was married three times by the time she was thirty-five, and we're pretty sure my uncle Ted's father is the milkman who swore he had an affair with granny off and on for years. Granny also could shoot a target dead-on when it was raining and she had only one eye open."

"Impressive."

"Now you're making fun of me."

He couldn't help it: he touched a strand of her hair that had fallen from her makeshift braid. "No, I've just never met anyone like you before."

"What, you've never met a woman who got stranded in a blizzard?"

"No, I've never met one who was so…alive." And it was true: they'd only met hours ago, and yet he'd felt a connection with her the first time she'd smiled. Everything about her radiated vitality. Holly could take on the world and laugh the entire time.

She didn't say anything, though. Her green eyes widened, and he wanted to kiss the freckles dotted across her cheeks.

As if sensing the tension in the room, Arya woofed at their feet, which effectively ended the moment.

"Um, you want a beer?" Matt stood up, taking their plates with him into the kitchen. At the sink, he almost stuck his head under the cold water to get himself to calm down.

Holly was staying with him because she had nowhere else to go. He wasn't going to take advantage of that fact. It didn't matter that he hadn't had sex in forever. It didn't matter that she was beautiful and sweet and her hair was like a flame.

"I'll just get a glass of water," she said as she walked into the kitchen.

He jumped, almost dropping the plate in his hand. Luckily,

she didn't seem to notice, but grabbed a glass from the cabinet like she'd lived here for ages.

Matt was about to tell her he was going to sleep—even though it was only seven o'clock—when the lights flickered and died, plunging the house into darkness.

CHAPTER TWO

Holly Cook stared into the darkness of Matt's house and reflected—rather wryly—that her thought that the night couldn't get any worse was being proven wrong with gusto.

She heard Matt curse, a dog woof, and then the sound of him hitting the corner of the coffee table.

"Dammit, Arya, Sansa, whoever you are, stay!" Matt practically growled. "I'm going to get a flashlight." He tromped off, the click of the dogs' nails following him.

When she'd left Louisiana two days ago, she hadn't had any destination in mind beyond getting away. She'd packed up her car and driven off, no course set, no idea of where she'd end up. She'd just gone north. Driving through Arkansas and then Missouri, she'd arbitrarily decided to stop in Kansas City when she'd gotten a flat…and then the blizzard hit.

What rotten luck, she thought with a sigh. Could she ever do anything without screwing it up? The answer was definitely *no*, she couldn't. Holly had dropped out of college her junior year, never finishing her degree, to run off with her then-boyfriend. She'd been twenty-one, in love, and stupid.

Now she was twenty-five, sick of love, and only a little bit wiser.

"Found it." Matt came into the living room, the beam of the flashlight bouncing off of the walls. The dogs barked; he shushed them and told them to go lie down on their giant dog beds in the corner.

Holly couldn't help smiling now. When she'd been stuck in that ditch, the snow falling all around her, she hadn't expected that anyone would be driving by, let alone a man like Officer Matthew Haldon. Tall, with dark hair, he wasn't what she'd classify as handsome, per se, but his face was kind, and he'd taken her into his home without protest. She hadn't known a lot of people who would be that kind to a stranger.

A small voice had whispered that she was crazy to go to a strange man's house, but he was a police officer, right? And looking at him, she felt like she could trust him.

She almost snorted at that thought. *Didn't you think the same thing about Sam?*

But she and Sam were over. Dunzo. She'd never see him again, and for that, she was infinitely thankful.

Matt switched on a battery-powered radio, which broadcasted the obvious news that there were power outages all over the state, and crews were working to get the power back on. He swore underneath his breath.

"It's below zero out there, and no electricity." He rubbed the back of his neck before looking over at Holly. "It's going to be a cold night, I'm afraid."

"Then I'm glad I took a hot shower before the power went out," she replied.

In all honesty, she'd experienced worse. Last year, when Sam had decided that they were going to save money and only spend ten dollars a week on food? She'd never been so hungry in her life. But Sam was like that: full of mad schemes, some that were brilliant, while the rest were completely insane. Holly had admired him for those schemes in the beginning. By the end of their relationship, she'd hated him for everything he'd put her through.

She shook off the memories. Right now, she was sitting next to a man who was so completely different from her ex that it was almost difficult to reconcile the two in her mind. Matt was…dependable. Staid. Solid. He probably had never schemed in his life.

Her lips turned up at the thought.

After getting the fire started, Matt sat back down next to her. He drew a blanket down from the couch and placed it on her shoulders. "You look cold," he said gruffly.

She clutched the blanket closer, staring up at him. He seemed to be looking at her mouth, she realized with a start. Turning away, he returned his gaze to the fire.

"So, tell me about yourself. You never answered my question," Holly said.

He raised an eyebrow. "You are persistent, you know that?"

"It's one of my best traits." She moved a little closer to him and patted his knee; that touch, though, sent electricity zinging through her hand and up her arm. Her body heating, she snatched her hand back and hid it underneath the blanket, like it had been branded.

No more touching Matthew Haldon, she told herself.

"Where did you go to school? What was your major? Do you prefer pies or cakes?" Holly chattered, throwing out random questions, trying to find her equilibrium. She couldn't look into his eyes right now. If she did, she was pretty sure she wouldn't find her way back.

Finally, he sighed. "You really want to know about me?"

She nodded.

"Well, let's see..." He rubbed the back of his neck, like he was embarrassed. "Like I said, I grew up in Illinois."

"Where in Illinois?"

"Springfield."

She nodded again. "What were you like as a kid? Shy? Outgoing? Bookish? Athletic?"

He barked out a laugh. "None of those things. I was just a kid. I played basketball briefly. I had okay grades, but nothing spectacular. That was my sister—she was the valedictorian. I had friends, I really liked PE..." He shrugged. "Look, I told you, I'm a boring guy."

Holly wasn't sure why she wanted to know these details about him. Maybe because he was so reticent to talk, so embarrassed by anyone being interested in him. She rubbed her hands together. If she were good at anything, it was getting people to talk.

"Okay, you know what we should do?" she asked.

"Should I even ask?"

"Let's play Truth or Dare."

He stared at her, and then he laughed that husky laugh that sent shivers down her spine. "Holly, this isn't some seventh grade girls' sleepover."

She ignored that. "You can start. Go on."

Leaning back against the couch, he assessed her. The fire crackled and a log collapsed in the grate, which made Holly jump.

"Okay, truth or dare?"

She smiled. "Truth."

"What's your favorite color?"

"That's a boring question! No, no, no, you have to ask something *juicy*. Come on, don't tell me you've never played!"

He let out a breath and thought for a moment. Waiting in anticipation, Holly set her chin on her hand.

"Fine," he said, "what did you want to be when you grew up?"

"Oh, that's easy. I wanted to be a unicorn."

"A unicorn."

"Yes, a unicorn."

"That's not exactly a *profession*."

"It is when you're four."

He stared at her, like she'd sprouted a unicorn horn right in his living room. Smiling widely, she explained, "My mom read *The Last Unicorn* to me when I was little, and after that, I decided I was going to become one. I told everyone who'd ask that that was what I was going to be when I grew up."

His gaze had softened, and her traitorous heart sped up at the look. "So why didn't you grow up to be a unicorn in the end?"

"Some kid told me they didn't exist, and that was that. My dream was dashed into pieces." She stared into the fire. It was silly, but she rather thought that that had been the first moment where she'd grown up. Before then, she'd believed she could become anything or anyone. After that, she'd had to learn the hard lesson of tempering expectations.

"Truth or dare," she asked him, wanting to push those memories away.

He considered. "Since I have a feeling you'll make me go outside and freeze, let's do truth."

"Who was your first kiss?"

To her amusement, a wash of red climbed up his cheeks. Or it could've just been from the reddish glow of the fire. She waited expectantly.

"Are we really talking about this—?" He sighed. "It was Danielle Hanson, third grade."

"Third grade!"

"She was my Valentine, you see." His voice was low, and Holly pulled her blanket closer to control her sudden shivering. "I gave her a Valentine, and she told me to meet her behind the slide at recess. She told me she wanted me to be her boyfriend, and I kissed her."

"What happened after that?"

He smiled wryly. "She stomped on my foot and said I was gross and to never kiss her again. So, my first love ended."

"Was your heart broken?"

He shook his head. "I had a new girlfriend a week later."

"For shame!" The dogs looked up at her rebuke, and she laughed. "Who knew that Officer Haldon was such a playboy?"

Now he was definitely blushing, which was intriguing. She'd gotten so used to Sam and his ilk that she'd forgotten there were people in this world who'd remained innocent. She'd lost her own innocence years ago, shed like a skin that had never fit her in the first place.

"Truth or dare?" Matt asked.

"Truth."

"Okay, who was your first kiss?"

She smiled at the memory. "Aaron Slater in sixth grade. He

was the most popular boy in school, and I'd had a crush on him the entire year. He asked me to the school dance, and then afterward, took me outside and kissed me."

Frowning, Matt replied, "I hope he only kissed you."

"We were twelve!" Indignant, she added, "We didn't even know how to kiss, let alone do anything else. Get your mind out of the gutter."

"Well, I wouldn't have blamed him if he'd tried to go further. I'm sure you were the prettiest girl in school."

To her surprise, a blush crawled up her cheeks. She looked away from his gaze, staring at the fire, which had been steadily fading as they'd talked. What time was it? What was she *doing?*

Matt grunted something and got up, and she wondered if she'd done something to offend him. But he just returned with a few beers, telling her they might as well drink something while they talked.

They bantered and revealed silly secrets from their pasts, and Holly discovered that Matt had missed his high school prom because he'd been suspended for a senior prank (it involved crickets and pigs set loose in the school), and that he'd almost given up his dream of becoming a police officer to take over his father's business when his father became ill.

"I'm the only son, but my parents never expected me to take over the business," he explained. "When my dad got cancer, things changed. I had to take off a year from school to keep things afloat. By the end, I wasn't sure if I'd even go back."

"What changed your mind?" she asked softly.

He smiled, but it was a sad smile. "My dad knew he didn't have much time left. He took me aside and said that there was no reason I should throw away my future because of him. So I didn't."

Holly wished she could tell a story like that about her parents, but she'd never known her father, and her mother was God only knew where right now. Holly's mom had dragged her from place to place, boyfriend to boyfriend, always looking for drugs and a place to sleep. By the time Holly had been in junior high, she'd run away enough times that the state put her in foster care. She'd left on her eighteenth birthday to attend college before she'd met Sam.

The conversation lulled, and Holly finished off her second beer and began on the third. She was pleasantly tipsy at the moment, and warm from the fire, the blanket, and the alcohol. She noticed that Matt had unbuttoned his shirt, which revealed a golden throat with light stubble dotting it. Wondering if he would taste as yummy as he looked, she willed herself not to reach out and touch him.

It's just been too long since you've had sex, her hazy mind reasoned. *Once you get on the road, you'll forget all about him.*

She had a distinct feeling that wouldn't be the case, but she was good at lying to herself. And her brain was too mushy to combat the idea, anyway.

"Tell me why you left Louisiana." Matt lifted his beer to his lips as he looked at her.

She swallowed. Sipping her own beer, she called herself all sorts of foolish for starting this game in the first place. Then again, there was a feeling of relief in the idea of spilling everything to this man. Would he understand, though? Or would he look at her in disgust instead of with his eyes flashing in the firelight?

"I broke up with my boyfriend a month ago," she said,

staring at the dancing flames of the fireplace. "But he wouldn't take no for an answer. Sam, he is—was—volatile. Emotional. We'd break up, and then he'd come back, begging for me to take him back. I always fell for it, but this time, I was done."

Matt just waited for her to continue.

"I got my own place and everything. I'd gotten a decent job down at the mall, and I was paying my rent. I'd never done that before—Sam had always done it. I'd changed my number, all the things they tell you to do. But he still found me."

Her voice fell away, and she sensed the tension running through Matt's body.

"What happened?" he asked softly.

She shrugged, but it was a pointless gesture. It was an attempt at levity where no levity could be found. "He came to my place, and we had a fight. A huge one. He…he pushed me up against the wall and tried to choke me."

Matt swore, and she looked at him in surprise. "That piece of shit," he growled. "I hope you killed him?"

She shook her head. "The cops came, and they took him away. But I knew that he'd get out on bail and find me. So I packed up my stuff and drove. I didn't even know where I'd go. And now I'm here, telling you my sob story."

"Holly." He looked like he wanted to touch her, but thought better of it. "I'm sorry."

"You know, it's funny. When people say that, I never believe them. I always think, 'why are they the ones saying sorry?' They didn't do anything. With you, I believe that you mean it."

They gazed at each other, and Holly felt her heart crack. Just a little—a mere fissure—but she wondered, with an overwhelming sadness, if the entire trajectory of her life could've been different if she'd met this man years earlier.

Now, though, it was simply too late. She wasn't going to get Matt involved in her troubles. She'd go underground, and forget any of this ever happened.

This was what she told herself, even though she knew with a painful clarity that it was a complete lie.

CHAPTER THREE

As the night waned on, Matt was aware of two pressing things: one, they were going to be out of firewood soon and the power hadn't come back on yet; and two, he was becoming more and more unwilling to part with Holly in the morning.

He watched as the fire slowly waned down to a mere spark, and he cursed himself for not getting more firewood before tonight. But who would have thought that the power would go out—and be out—this long? It had been close to three hours now, and the house was beginning to get colder, but nothing dire yet. He glanced at Holly, wrapped up in her blankets, and his very stupid mind told him he wouldn't mind sharing body warmth with her if necessary.

Leave her alone, he told himself. *She's been through hell and back again. She doesn't need you getting handsy.*

This was what Matt told himself, but it didn't stop the thoughts from pouring into his mind. He couldn't sleep now. How could he sleep with her sitting next to him, smelling of flowers, her bright red hair glinting in the low light?

He saw her shiver. "You want another blanket?" he asked.

She rubbed her arms underneath the blanket around her. "I'm just so cold," she said softly, like it surprised her. "Do you think they'll get the power on anytime soon?"

Considering they were out in the middle of nowhere…he doubted it. The storm raged on outside, and although he could maybe try to drive into town if he were desperate enough, he could also end up in a ditch like Holly, and then he'd been in real trouble. He couldn't very well go out into the blizzard to chop down wood for the fire, either. So he got up, grabbed all of the blankets and comforters he had, and wrapped the fuzziest one around Holly's thin shoulders.

"Come and sit with me," he said, not even thinking about what he was saying. If she was cold, he could warm her. It would be silly not to share warmth. "I'm basically a human furnace."

She hesitated, but after a moment of indecision, she scooted toward him. She didn't sit right next to him, though, like they were in junior high on their first date. He couldn't help but smile.

"I won't bite, I promise."

She laughed softly. Moving until her thigh pressed against his, she curled up against him. Matt wrapped his arm around her, and he couldn't help the feeling that this was *right*. She fit perfectly against him.

"Better?" His voice was husky, low. If he didn't know better, they were lovers, sitting together in front of the fire on a winter's night.

She looked up at him, her lashes dark, and she said in a voice that sent a shiver through him, "Better."

He wanted to kiss her. He wanted to kiss her so badly he

felt it in his bones. He wanted to protect her and keep her safe from everyone who would try to hurt her, and he wanted to make her smile and laugh. He wanted to tell her about his boring life and have her tell him that he wasn't boring, but that he had as much to offer as anyone else.

Reaching up to stroke her cheek, he reveled when she didn't push him away. She just stared up at him, her gaze unreadable in the dim light, and he touched the silky softness of her cheek. He pushed a strand of her hair off of her forehead. He touched her hair. And then he leaned down, not thinking, just feeling—and wanting.

"Matt..." She turned her face away. Was she breathing harder, or was it his imagination? "We can't."

His heart plummeted to his toes. What the hell was he doing? Did he really take women home and then try to kiss them when they had nowhere else to go? Disgust filled him, but only directed at himself.

When Holly tried to move away, he said, "I'm sorry. I'm an idiot. But I don't want you to freeze." She didn't say anything, so he added, "I won't touch you again. I promise."

He saw a bit of a smile on her face. "It's not that I don't want you to, but I can't. I'm too messed up. There's too much of...everything." She looked up at him again. "You know what I mean?"

He did, and he didn't. But he nodded, and they stared into the dying fire, and Matt told himself when the snow stopped, he'd let her go. He'd let her go, and he'd never see her again.

But the snow raged on, and on, piling up outside, and when the fire completely went out, the house was plunged into darkness and frigid temperatures. Matt wished he hadn't been cheap, deciding against a back-up generator. When he got up to go to the bathroom, he saw that the outside thermometer read 0 degrees Fahrenheit. He turned on the radio when he got back, and the weather report didn't help him feel better.

"The snow will continue into the night and the morning," the weatherman said in a bland voice. "Thousands are currently without power, and crews are working into the night to restore electricity. That being said, visibility is so poor that I imagine a lot of you won't have any power for some time yet. Stay warm, folks."

Matt switched off the radio. Holly snuggled against him, but he soon felt her shivering again. He refused to let her get cold like that.

"Come on, let's go upstairs to my room," he said. When she just froze, he blushed. "Not for *that*. I mean, because it'll be warmer upstairs, and we can wrap up in the blankets on a bed instead of the couch."

"Are you sure?" Holly sounded dubious.

"Very. Arya, Sansa, come on. Let's take all of these blankets upstairs, and we'll make a cocoon out of them. We can also stuff the cracks in the windows so we don't lose all of the residual heat. I also have plenty of socks and jackets, too."

Holly followed him upstairs, carrying blankets, the dogs padding behind them. Although Arya and Sansa were never allowed on the bed, Matt let them get up there with them since they were basically large heaters, and he hated to think of the dogs shivering in the cold on the floor. He stuffed the cracks in the windows, shut the bedroom door, and wrapped himself up in blankets. Holly put on layers of socks and mittens and a hat, and he couldn't help but smile at her when she got on the bed with him.

He held his arms out to her. This time, she didn't hesitate. She burrowed against him, sighing contentedly.

"How are you so warm?" Her breath fanned against his throat.

"I think I run hotter than most people. Or it's just all of my muscles, you know."

She laughed, and his body heated at the sound. "Something like that, I'm sure."

He was all too aware of her against him, her body sweet and soft, and he cursed himself when his body reacted. He just hoped that with all of the blankets and clothes between them that she was unaware of the hardness against her. The last thing she needed was some creep poking her in the stomach with his erection when they were in a life or death situation.

Okay, it maybe wasn't life or death, all things considered, but still. He'd already gone too far in touching her; making her aware how much he wanted her? That was something else entirely.

She breathed against his throat, her eyelashes fluttering. Within minutes, she fell asleep, and he thanked God for it. *May she sleep the night away,* he thought. *May she wake up, and the power is back on, and then I can get her car out and on her way.*

Arya snored behind him, while Sansa was lying against Holly's back. All in all, the two humans and two canines were toasty warm. Feeling exhaustion swamp his limbs, it wasn't long before Matt fell asleep, too.

IT WAS STILL DARK when Matt awoke to a noise that he first thought was one of the dogs fretting to get out. He opened his eyes, trying to make anything out in the gloom, when he realized that it wasn't one of the dogs. It was Holly. She whimpered and moaned, pushing against his chest, and she kept saying something.

"Please don't," she pleaded, pushing and pushing. "Please. Sam, you can't. *Please!*"

Matt froze. Did he wake her, or let the dream play out? He didn't want to startle her. But when she started trying to hit him, he didn't have much of a choice.

He shook her. "Holly! Holly, wake up! It's a dream, sweetheart." He didn't even realize the endearment had fallen from his lips, but it felt right for some reason. "Holly, wake up. Wake up."

She moaned. He almost thought she'd fallen back asleep, but her lashes fluttered and then she looked up at him like he was a stranger. He couldn't make out her expression in the dark, so he switched on the flashlight.

They both blinked at the bright light. Finally, he was able to see her face, and he realized with a start that she'd been crying.

"Oh Holly," he breathed. He brushed a tear from her cheek. "What were you dreaming?"

She shuddered; he pulled her close. Arya snuffled, her snout almost in his armpit.

"It was nothing. Sometimes I have weird dreams." But her voice was shaky.

"Tell me what happened. Was it about your ex? Sam?"

She shook her head.

"You said his name," he said gently. "You kept saying *please* and *no*, too."

She seemed to deflate in his arms, like she didn't have the energy even to speak now.

"I keep having dreams," she finally whispered into the gloom. "About when Sam attacked me. I thought by now I'd be over it, but it's like every time I close my eyes, he's there. Sometimes I get away, but other times, I don't."

He rubbed her back in soothing circles, rage filling him. If he could get his hands on this Sam character, he would. He'd punch him so hard he'd see stars, and then he'd punch him again for good measure. How could someone treat someone as lovely and caring as Holly so badly? He'd seen enough domestic violence cases as a police officer to know there was no rhyme or reason to them, besides men wanting to hurt women and not let them get away.

He felt her body shudder, and she cried against his shoulder. He let her, not knowing what else to do. Despite feeling helpless, he rubbed her back and said soothing words into her hair. To his relief, it seemed to help calm her down after some time.

She moved so she could wipe her face. "God, I'm sorry," she said. "Here I am, making you take me to your house, feeding me, and then I end up crying like a baby. You must think I'm insane."

"Not insane. Just scared. And sad."

She bit her lip before letting out a breath. "I'm so tired of being scared," she admitted. "So tired, Matt. What if he finds me? He'll kill me. I know he will. What if I can never get away from him?"

He shushed her, but he didn't tell her she shouldn't be afraid. He knew the statistics; he'd seen the aftermath more than once. Not in Heron's Landing, but when he'd first started working as a cop. He'd go out to one place in particular, see the bruises on that woman's face, but her husband had somehow managed to avoid jail time. And when she'd tried to leave… He forced the memories away. This time, he'd keep this woman in his arms safe from harm.

Holly sighed. Matt kissed her forehead, even though he knew he shouldn't. But it wasn't a sexual kiss, but one of comfort. A promise. *I won't let anything happen to you.*

When she tipped her head back, her eyes dark, he didn't stop her when she touched his face. When she brushed finger-tips across his eyebrows, down his face, tracing the line of his jaw. She smiled a little at the feeling of his stubble. He barely breathed when her thumb brushed his lower lip. And when she reached up and pressed her mouth against his, he didn't tell her that this wasn't a good idea. He didn't say anything at all.

Instead, he wrapped her in his arms, and he kissed her with everything he had, because it was the only response that made sense. She made sense. He slanted his mouth over hers, tasting her sweetness, and when she moaned? His heart thrilled.

He kissed her until his mind emptied. Gentle, teasing kisses, kisses that told her everything he'd wanted to say the moment he'd first seen her. Kisses that even he didn't fully comprehend. Kisses that made him see stars behind his eyelids.

He felt fingers in his hair, and he laughed a little when Holly pulled off the ski cap he'd put over his hair. What did he need all of these clothes and blankets for anyway? He was an inferno. He was burning up. It was like a fever underneath his skin, but it was a fever solely for this woman in his arms.

Holly touched her tongue to his, and it was like flame to kindling. He rolled her over, kissing her all the while, their bodies aligned. His erection pressed against her thigh, and she whispered his name as they kissed harder and harder. He wouldn't be surprised if steam was rising from their bodies. Their tongues dancing together, he touched her face, her neck, wishing he could get her out of all of these damn clothes—

And then he heard a whir and suddenly, the house came alive. The power turned back on, the heat practically bursting through the vents. Arya and Sansa barked, running from the bed, and the light flooding the room caused Matt to realize what they were doing. That he was on top of Holly, that they'd been kissing, and that he was the biggest jackass this side of the Mississippi.

Holly's face seemed to echo his own horror, and he sat up so quickly that he felt dizzy. But they were still entangled in all of those damn blankets, and he cursed when he couldn't free himself. Holly finally stumbled from the bed, her hair a mess, and then she ran from the room like the hounds of hell were at her heels.

Matt collapsed back into the bed. Eventually, Arya and Sansa came back, licking his dangling fingers. He patted them on the head, muttering, "I'm such an idiot," to no one in particular.

CHAPTER FOUR

Holly shut the door to the guest bedroom and promptly collapsed in front of said door, her heart pounding so hard she felt dizzy. She still had one of the blankets wrapped around her shoulders, and she shrugged it off and tossed it into a corner somewhere. The heat blazed through the house now that the power had come back on; it was so loud that Holly could almost imagine she was alone.

Of course, she wasn't alone—not even slightly. She thought about Matt: about his kisses, and touches, and how he smelled so good. Why did he have to smell so good? It wasn't fair. She wished an old man with two teeth and who smelled like fish had picked her up out of that stupid ditch. Then she wouldn't be sitting here, her hand over her heart, wanting to return to Matt's room and kiss him again.

I can't let this happen, she told herself. Matt didn't need to get caught up in her drama, and besides, she had terrible judgment in men. When she'd first met Sam, she'd thought he was the sun, the moon, and the stars. She'd loved him—and trusted him—within a day of meeting him. And look how that had turned out. Running for her life from the very man she'd been convinced was her soulmate.

So, no, she couldn't very well throw herself at the next available man, even if he was delicious, and kind, and kissed like a god. Holly groaned, slumping to the floor. She relived those kisses, over and over again, until she wanted to scratch out her very brain. If only he had been a terrible kisser! All slobbery and with bad breath.

It would be her luck that a man like Matt would be the one to save her, wouldn't it?

She lay on the floor, staring up at the ceiling. Dawn was finally approaching, and rays of light shown through the windows as the sun rose. She glanced out the window. The snow was slowing down, and soon, Matt would take her back to her car, and she'd get on her way. To where, she wasn't really sure. Kansas City had been a vague destination, one that had seemed far, far away from Sam and Louisiana.

She rubbed her eyes. She wanted to stay here, with Matt, but how could she? What if Sam showed up at his doorstep? Or what if her infamous bad judgment revealed that Matt wasn't as great a guy as she'd thought?

Okay, yes, he was a cop. And he'd helped her without even asking for anything, and he'd stopped touching her when she'd freaked out. And he hadn't run after her when she'd run out of his bedroom, yelling at her that she was a tease. He hadn't done anything that would make her think he was like Sam.

And yet...

Holly sighed. Her heart slowed down, until she felt like she could breathe again, but her body tingled despite her best efforts. She pressed a finger against her lip; she closed her eyes.

She'd give herself five minutes: five minutes to relive Matt's kisses and touch. Going to her bag, she pulled out her phone and set the timer. Then she got onto the guest bed, lay down, and remembered. She remembered his smell, and how he said her name in that husky voice of his, and how he'd tempted her with kisses that had been seduction itself. How his weight had felt on top of her; how he'd touched her—so gently, almost reverently. How he'd tasted of beer and what she'd come to recognize as Matt. Matt, Matt, Matt.

The timer sounded. She picked up her phone, silencing it, before closing her eyes and wishing she knew what to do next.

THE SNOW HAD STOPPED COMPLETELY by morning. Holly ventured downstairs early in the morning, but when Matt had entered the kitchen, she'd turned coward and scampered back to her room.

Now, though, she was starving, and she needed coffee rather desperately. Going back downstairs, she didn't see Matt at all, until she rounded the corner and saw that he was digging out his driveway. She watched him for a moment, his arms and shoulders strong, his nose red from the cold. He'd already made a serious dent in the snow, although she couldn't imagine he'd be able to clear his entire driveway—a seemingly endless driveway that finally emptied onto the country road west of it—but then again, he was a determined man. She had a feeling he could manage just about anything if he set his mind to it.

Arya came up then and nosed at her hand, the coldness of the dog's nose startling her. She laughed, and Arya barked as Sansa joined her.

"Come on, you two. Let's get me some food before I end up doing something really stupid."

Holly made herself some scrambled eggs with a steaming cup of coffee. She listened to the house creak, the dogs woofing softly at her feet, and she could hear Matt shoveling snow as she ate. She didn't know what she was going to say when he came inside. *Sorry, we shouldn't have kissed? Sorry, I'm an idiot? Sorry, you're a good guy but I'm a mess?*

She reached down and gave the dogs a bite of egg, which they received with the expected doggy enthusiasm. "What the hell am I doing?" she asked them. They just wagged their tails in unison.

Matt finally came back inside before lunchtime, sweaty and smelling like a man who'd gotten in a good workout. Holly rather loved that smell, and her heart thrilled when he walked past her in the kitchen. His dark hair was mussed, his shoulders rippling beneath his shirt that had been under his thick coat. He filled a glass of water without saying anything to her, drinking one glass and then another in quick gulps.

She got down from her stool, about to let him be alone, but his voice stopped her.

"We better go get your car."

She turned to look at him. He didn't seem particularly fazed, and for some reason, that irritated her. Shouldn't he feel as awkward as she after what had happened? Or did he just not care? She gripped her mug of coffee harder.

"Do you think that's a good idea? Can we even get out of here?" She raised an eyebrow.

"I have four-wheel drive, and they'll have plowed the road. It'll be snow-packed, but not impassable. Are you okay driving, though?"

She wanted to tell him the last thing she wanted to do was drive on snow-packed country roads, but he didn't seem particularly inclined to have her stay as a guest. Her shoulders slumped. She couldn't really blame him. Here she was, telling him to leave her alone one moment, and the next, she was practically throwing herself at him. Would she never learn?

"I'll go get my stuff."

She tossed her things into her bag and met him outside. When he handed her his coat, she balked.

"It's an old one," he explained over her protestations. "Take it. I'm not going to let you go off without a coat, Holly."

The drive to her car was slow, Matt taking his time, and Holly inhaled his scent with every breath. She wished she could say something to break the tension, but what could she do? But when she glanced at him out of the corner of her eye, she saw that he was frowning, and her initial frustration with him melted away like so much snow against the hot car.

"I'm sorry," she said, not looking at him. "I've given you so much trouble. But I appreciate everything you've done, for what it's worth."

He took a deep breath, tapping his fingers against the steering wheel. "You don't have to apologize. It was my fault as much as yours."

She opened her mouth to deny that, but then she thought better of it. She chewed her lip, wishing she could find the right words to explain…everything.

"When I first met Sam, I thought he was amazing," she said softly. She could see Matt stiffen, but he didn't tell her to stop talking, either. "He was like a whirlwind, you know? All emotion and energy. That night, I had told him that I'd never had a pet growing up, and he thought that was a great tragedy. I laughed at his antics. But the next morning, he showed up at my door with a tiny kitten with a ribbon wrapped around its neck." Holly sighed at the memory. "I had no idea how to take care of a kitten, and I didn't have the money for it, either. But the gesture was so sweet that I knew right then and there that I'd fallen in love with him."

Matt was still tapping his fingers against the steering wheel. "Where's the cat now?"

Holly looked out the window at the snow-covered land. "After I moved in with Sam, he constantly complained about the cat. He hated it. It got fur all over his stuff, and it howled at night, and he told me that if I didn't get rid of it, he would." She wiped her eyes at the memory. "So I had to take it to a shelter, because Sam didn't want it anymore."

"That's a shitty thing to make someone do."

"Yes, it was. But I'm telling you this because I don't have good judgment. I think a person is good, and safe, and kind, but they always turn out to be something else as time passes. No matter how hard I look, I somehow end up being wrong." Her eyes watered; she told herself it was from the brightness of the sun against the white snow. "I'm just too screwed up," she finally said into the quiet.

Matt was silent. She didn't know if he understood her, or if he thought she was being ridiculous, or if he didn't care. She wanted him to say something, though. What was he thinking? Did he regret what had happened this morning?

"The problem with your story," he said quietly, "is that you're blaming yourself for other people's actions. Judgment is one thing, but expecting others to act decently doesn't make you weak. It makes you human."

She looked at him now, memorizing the lines of his face. His dear, handsome face. He turned so their gazes met.

"Don't let that hope in others ever leave you, because as a cop, I can tell you that it's a difficult thing to hold onto," he said.

They fell silent as they approached her car. She helped him dig it out, as it was covered in so much snow that you'd almost miss it if you weren't looking for it. The work gave her a respite from her thoughts, although she couldn't help but watch as Matt worked.

Finally, they'd cleared the snow enough that he could replace the flat tire, although she had to help him get her stuff out of the trunk so he could get to the spare. He changed the tire so quickly she hadn't even realized he was done until he started placing her things back inside the car.

She got inside, feeling tears press at her eyelids. This was goodbye, wasn't it? She didn't know where she could even go, not really. She only had a little money. Biting the inside of her cheek, she forced herself not to cry like a baby in front of Matt. He'd done enough. He didn't have to save her from this, too.

"Follow me, okay?" he said before she closed the car door.

She nodded, not sure why she needed to follow him, but she supposed it could get easy to get lost in all of this snow.

They drove slowly, Holly following two cars behind him as he'd advised her. She cranked up the heat in her car, glad that she'd filled up her gas tank not long ago. She turned on the radio, but the cheery sound of Christmas music only made her more depressed. Switching it off, she decided that silence was better than a false attempt at cheer.

As they drove down the road, she watched as Matt turned. She followed, frowning. Why was he taking her back to his house? Had she forgotten something? She drove very slowly behind him until she reached his garage. She parked her car and got out at the same time he did.

"What is it?" She walked up to him, confusion marring her features. "Did I forget something?"

He glanced at her, surprised. "Did you really think I was going to let you go on your own when your ex could be following you?" His voice seemed incredulous, like she'd just told him the moon was really made of cheese.

She blinked. Well, she had thought that, hadn't she? "Why?" was all she could say.

"Holly, I'm a cop. I'm going to help you get away from this guy." He touched her arm, his expression gentle. "I'm not going to give you a cat and then force you to get rid of it."

It didn't make any sense, not really, and yet, those words sent a thrill through her. A thrill that soon transformed into tears that wouldn't stop flowing. Matt had turned away from her already, and she was glad of that. She didn't want him to see how weak she really was. She wanted him to think she could handle herself, no matter what happened.

They entered the house, the dogs barking, and Holly hugged herself. She hoped her judgment was right this time. She hoped it so hard that her heart almost burst.

Seeing Matt look at her, a small smile on his face, she could almost tell herself everything would be okay. She didn't need to be afraid anymore.

"Thank you." She took his hands, smiling up at him. "Thank you for everything."

He seemed to want to reach out to touch her face, but he didn't. He stood back, nodded, and went into the kitchen without so much as a backward glance.

CHAPTER FIVE

When Matt drove Holly back to her car, he'd wrestled with what he should do. Should he let her go, never see her again, and hope for the best? He had a feeling that was what she thought *she* should do. What claim did she have on him, and vice versa?

But his honor clawed at him, and he knew that he couldn't let her go with her ex out there, the ex that could—and very likely would—hurt her given half the chance. Matt was a police officer and had access to things that a normal citizen wouldn't. What kind of a man would let a woman like Holly leave as he sat back and did nothing?

So after he'd changed her tire and they'd driven back to his place, he told her that he wouldn't let her leave until she was safe to do so. The look of surprise on her face had both amused and frustrated him. It also saddened him that she automatically expected that people wouldn't help her, at least nothing beyond the essentials.

He watched as she went back inside his house. He decided to make some calls, find out as much as he could about Sam.

Refusing to let Holly drive away was something any man with a conscience would do. It had nothing to do with how much he wanted her, or how he couldn't stop thinking about how she'd felt against him last night.

He grimaced at the memory while his body heated. He shouldn't think about it; he should let it go. But her kisses and her moans would stay with him for years to come. She'd awakened something in him, something that wasn't just lust, but something that he hadn't felt since he'd first met Melanie. That desire for connection, for a relationship, for *love*.

He shook himself. He couldn't do this. He could help Holly, but nothing beyond that. When she was safe, he'd let her go.

"I'm going to get some work done," he told her as she sat down with a cup of coffee in the living room. "I'm going to call some guys, get some information about that ex of yours. What's his last name?"

Holly hesitated, but eventually she gave in. "Sam Gantry, born in Chicago on August 1, 1981," she rattled off. "I can give you his social security number, his phone number, address— the works."

Matt pulled out his notepad and scribbled down everything she told him, making mental notes as he did so. He knew that restraining orders were just pieces of paper, but it would be a start. If he could pull some strings and get one processed before Christmas, it would be a miracle.

"Did you ever report his assaults to the police down in Louisiana?"

She grimaced. "Only once. The neighbors called the cops on us that last time, and I gave them a statement. They took me back to the station for photos and stuff, but he ended up not getting out on bail." She rolled her eyes. "Go figure."

Matt grunted. He was all too aware of how these guys somehow managed to avoid jail time. It didn't help that these cases often ended up as he-said, she-said, ignoring the fact that women lying about domestic violence was extremely rare.

He took some more notes and then headed upstairs. He knew a few guys down in Louisiana, one of whom he'd worked with his first year on the force. Calling up Dan, Matt gave him the details of the case, asking him if he could look further into Sam Gantry's rap sheet. If they could hang the guy on any charge, Matt would take it. He didn't care if it was jaywalking—anything would do. Anything to keep him from coming after Holly and enacting revenge for her leaving.

"It says here that this guy was arrested for public intoxication just a week ago," Dan said in his Southern drawl. "He got out on bail, but he has a court date for mid-January."

"Can the date be pushed up?"

Dan snorted. "I'm not a judge, dude, but based on all of this, Ms. Cook can definitely file a restraining order, no problem. That would at least be a start."

"And what happens when this guy decides he doesn't give two shits about a piece of paper saying to stay 500 feet away?"

"We all know it's just a detail, but at least if he gets close, you can arrest him." Dan was typing in the background. "I'll get you the paperwork here in an hour, and then if you get her signature, we can hopefully get this done before everything closes down for Christmas."

"Thanks, Dan. I really appreciate it."

"This woman must have really made an impression on you."

Matt stared at his keyboard, unsure how to respond. Finally, he said, "Just trying to help someone down on her luck."

Dan didn't contradict him, and they said their goodbyes. Within the hour, Dan sent over the paperwork, and Matt went straight downstairs to have Holly sign them.

"I know it's not a huge thing," he said, almost apologetically, "but at least if he gets close, we can do something about it."

She nodded, her face drawn, signing the documents without comment. But as he was about to go upstairs, she touched his arm. "Thank you. For everything."

He smiled. "Just doing my job, madam."

She didn't smile back, though, and his heart hurt seeing it. After he sent everything back to Dan, his fellow officer assured him he'd do everything in his power to get everything completed before Christmas. It was all Matt could do for the time being, at any rate.

The day dragged on, and it was evening when Holly knocked at his office door. "Doing okay up here?"

He turned toward her, and he once again marveled at how lovely she was. That creamy skin, and red hair, and her flushed cheeks. The dogs sat on their haunches next to her, and he couldn't help but wonder what it would be like to have her around all the time. As a girlfriend, fiancée. Wife. He pushed that thought way back, knowing it could never happen.

"Dan told me that he should get everything to the judge and we'll have that restraining order finally." Matt got up and pet Arya behind her ears. "But I think you should stay here for the time being."

"So you'll keep me locked up in a tower for the rest of my life?" Holly smiled sadly.

"No, but if you're alone, and Sam finds you, what happens then?" Matt pushed a hand through his hair. "How will you protect yourself?"

"I just won't let him find me."

"Do you really think it's that easy? Holly, I've seen what happens on these cases. I've seen the aftermath. These guys don't just give up." He stared at her, trying to get her to see sense. "If you get hurt on my watch, I'll never forgive myself."

To his surprise, Holly embraced him, laying her face against his chest. "You don't have to protect the entire world," she murmured. "I knew what I was facing when I left him. I knew that he'd be more dangerous as a result." Looking up at him, she said, "You can't keep everyone safe, and I can't stay here forever."

He wrapped his arms around her. "If you staying here forever is what needs to happen, then that's what I'll do."

She shook her head, but she didn't tell him no, either.

She eventually pulled away. "You know what we need to do?"

He raised an eyebrow.

"Put up your Christmas tree. How is it that it's two days from Christmas and you haven't put anything up?"

He hadn't even thought about Christmas decorations this year, if he were being honest. Melanie had always done them. But this year, he hadn't been thinking about Melanie, or Christmas.

He'd been thinking about Holly.

Holly had somehow managed to find the Christmas tree and ornaments stacked in the basement, and he helped her haul them up the stairs. He took the tree from her and tossed it over his shoulders, the dogs barking at their antics.

"You realize this will all be coming down in three days, right?" he said as they went into the living room.

She just grinned. "You're such a party pooper. Now get that tree out of the box and we'll get this place looking like Christmas."

Holly's enthusiasm was infectious, he had to admit. He helped her put the tree together, a plastic thing from Walmart he'd bought ages ago, and although it looked rather scraggly, he enjoyed helping Holly decorate it. Turning on some Christmas music, they hung the tree with lights as Arya and Sansa attempted to help. When only some of the lights even turned on, Holly laughed.

"That is the saddest looking tree I've ever seen."

"Hey, it's been through a lot," Matt said as he fiddled with the lights. "Be nice to it."

"I'm not sure it's going to make much of a difference."

They finally got enough lights on there to make it look like a real Christmas tree, and then began the arduous task of hanging ornaments. For the most part, Matt only had plastic colored balls, but he had a few sentimental ornaments from his childhood that his mom had given him in the years past.

Holly held up a basketball ornament. "Yours?"

"Of course. Oh, and this one." He held up a snowman police officer, which just made Holly laugh.

Seeing Holly laughing and happy, Matt could only wish this would last. How had he fallen so hard for someone he'd just met a day before? But that was surely madness, wasn't it? He was probably just projecting; he was lonely; he hadn't had sex in too long. Once she left, he'd get his head back on straight, and he could get back to his life.

Holly made them both hot chocolate spiked with peppermint schnapps, and they sipped their mugs as they gazed at the Christmas tree. "Let It Snow" came on the radio, and if Matt closed his eyes, he could almost imagine they were a real family.

Looking down at Holly, he couldn't help but reach out and touch her. Feel the silk of her hair, and see her eyes widen slightly. Her lips parted, and when she didn't pull away, he kissed her. She tasted like peppermint.

He kissed her as the music flowed around them and the lights flickered and as his heart pounded and told him that he'd be a fool to let her go.

"I want you to stay," he murmured against her mouth. "Stay with me, Holly."

"Oh, Matt."

"I know you think you can't, or you think you have to leave. You don't. We have something here. I know you feel it as much as I do."

She looked at her feet, biting her lip. Matt's heart pounded, waiting for her answer.

"I want to, but I just can't." She sighed. "I wish I could, though."

He didn't understand her answer. He wanted to rail at her. Was she still in love with her ex? No, that wasn't it. She thought she deserved to be alone? That made the most sense, perhaps.

He grabbed her hand. "At least think about it."

She stilled. She didn't pull away, but she didn't say anything, either.

They both went to their separate bedrooms that night, although both dogs followed Holly into her room before Matt got them to come with him. He and Holly didn't say much of anything else that evening. With the restraining order still not complete, he'd told her she should stay put for now, to which she'd nodded and agreed.

Now, Matt lay in bed, staring up at the ceiling. He couldn't sleep, not with Holly just a few doors away, lying in her own bed. Was this love? He didn't know. He'd loved Melanie, but that had been a slow, almost easy-going kind of love, a love that had left its sting but hadn't broken him. This, though, whatever this was with Holly? It didn't compare. It was like trying to compare a candle with a fiery blaze.

Finally, he fell asleep, dreaming of Holly and her bright red hair. He didn't know how long he'd fallen asleep when something woke him up. A movement? A sound? His heart beating fast, he told himself he'd been dreaming, but he couldn't get the thought that something had happened out of his mind.

When he rose from the bed and flipped on his lamp, Sansa woofed quietly. Both dogs got up to help him investigate, their tails wagging. He looked at the clock: 3:05 AM. The sun wouldn't rise for some hours yet, of course. He yawned, considering getting something to drink.

Passing by Holly's room, he almost knocked on her door. But he'd be a huge jerk to wake her up, and besides, what would he say? "I woke up for some reason and decided to wake you up, too?" He pressed his ear against her door, and to his surprise, it wasn't latched. The door swung open, creaking, and he winced.

He waited for Holly to wake up, ask him what the hell he was doing, but the light from his own room filtering into the hallway showed that Holly's room was empty. Arya got up onto the bed and began digging in the sheets before curling up where Holly had been sleeping.

He flipped on the light, and he saw that her coat and boots were gone. His heart pounding, he raced downstairs, calling out her name. "Holly! Holly, where are you?" He knew the answer, but he wanted to make sure. Maybe she'd moved to the living room. Maybe she was sleepwalking. Maybe a meteor had hit earth and he was in some alternate universe.

He went straight into the garage, and seeing Holly's car was gone, he cursed a blue streak. The restraining order wasn't even complete, and she'd decided to take off? Arya came up beside him and nosed at his hand.

"She's gone, buddy," he said in a low voice. "I guess she couldn't stay here any longer."

Anger surged through him. Not so much at her, but at the situation. What if her ex found her? What if he traced her to her destination and hurt her? Matt had to push away the panic, but he knew the fear was justified. Sam was a dangerous man—so why had Holly left in the first place?

He tried calling her, but he got no answer. He left a voice-mail—*Please call me back right away*—and then sent her a text asking her to do the same. Finally, unable to calm himself, he got dressed, grabbed his gear, and set off to find her.

Driving to the main road, he stopped to see if he could tell which direction she'd gone, but there were too many tracks already in the snow. He decided to go north, which had been her original direction in the first place. This country road lasted for some miles before branching out into two highways: one that continued north, and the other that went east or west. Would she still continue on to Kansas City, or would she try another route?

Gripping the steering wheel, Matt only prayed that he caught up to her before her ex did.

CHAPTER SIX

As Holly got ready for bed and wondered what the hell she was going to do next, she heard her phone ring. The number was Unknown; seeing it, her heart pounded. She'd changed her number a second time since leaving Louisiana, but had Sam found her anyway?

She let the call go to voicemail. They didn't leave a message, but they kept calling. And calling. Then the texts started pouring in. *Where the fuck r u, what the fuck is wrong w u, do u rly think ur getting away?*

She knew exactly who it was. Sam. He'd found her. She didn't know how, but if he'd gotten her phone number, could he find her location, too? She didn't know what he was capable of.

Her phone rang once again, but she didn't pick up. She was about to turn her phone off and toss it into the snow when she got another text message: *I know where u r. U can come back, or u will be sorry. U and everyone around u.*

She started trembling. If Sam had found out about the restraining order, she was in deep, deep shit. He'd take that as a challenge to find her and hurt her, only to prove that he could. She knew the statistics, and she knew that abusers were often more dangerous after you left them than when you stayed. She'd been so stupid, she realized, trying to stifle a sob. How could she really have thought that Sam would leave her alone?

But it was the last text message that made her shake so hard her teeth chattered: *Come outside Holly. I know ur in there. I saw u putting up that Christmas tree. U already find another guy to do what u want?*

He was here. *He was here.* How was he here? She listened, shaking, and she knew that if she told Matt, Sam would go ballistic. He'd kill Matt—and she knew Matt was a cop, but he wasn't impervious to bullets, either—and then what?

She waited until Matt went into his bedroom and shut the door. Then she put on the coat he'd given her and stuffed her feet into her boots, her body still trembling. She didn't cry, though. The tears had all dried up ages ago. She stepped quietly down the stairs and out the backdoor. Walking toward the snow-covered field in the back of the house, she knew that Sam would find her.

He always did.

"Look who finally came out to play." His voice was silky, seemingly calm.

Holly turned to see the man she thought she'd loved standing in front of her: with his shaggy blond hair and blue eyes, he seemed harmless enough. He looked more like a surfer, the type who preferred sun and sand rather than hurting his girlfriends. But he had a dark side, which Holly was all too aware of.

She hugged herself close, her breath puffing in the cold. "What do you want?"

"Not even a hug? I came all the way here for you and you act like this?"

"I didn't ask you to come here." She tipped her chin up. "How did you find me anyway?"

Sam shrugged. "It was easy enough once I got your phone number. GPS is a handy thing, you know. And you are aware your phone bill is still attached to *my* account, right?" At her expression, he laughed. "So it was just a case of using 'find your phone' and voila! There you are." He patted her arm, like she was a silly child. "At least you tried, darling."

She shook off his hand. "I don't want anything to do with you. Haven't you figured that out by now? We're over. We were over when you tried to *choke* me."

He frowned. "That was an accident. I didn't mean to hurt you, but you made me so mad. Come on, don't hold a grudge against me. We've both fucked up."

"I've never tried to choke you, Sam."

His eyes narrowed, and Holly knew she was playing with fire. If she got him angry enough, there was no telling what he'd do. "It's freezing out here, and you really want to argue the details?" He grabbed her arm, and she almost shouted for Matt. But Sam gripped her tighter and hissed in her ear, "Make another sound, and your new boyfriend is dead. You think he'll really save you? I'll shoot him through the heart before you can scream." He shook her like a rag doll. "Now shut up and come with me."

She saw that Sam hadn't driven himself as they got to the garage. He demanded her keys, which she handed over with a great amount of reluctance.

"How did you get here?" she couldn't help but ask.

"I drove, but then I hitched a ride out here. Wouldn't want to be traced, and besides, using your car will make it look like you left on your own." Sam didn't turn on the engine, but instead put the car in neutral and slowly backed out of the driveway. It wasn't until they were some distance from the house that he turned the car on, and heat filled the vehicle. It didn't help Holly's shaking, but at least she wouldn't freeze to death.

"Now," Sam said as he smiled over at her, "where should we go?"

"You don't know?"

He made a face, and before she could react, he slapped her across the face. Her cheek stinging, she bit her lip to keep from crying.

"You talk like that to me again, and you'll get worse." Sam turned so they headed north, and Holly prayed that Matt would find them before they got too far.

BEFORE THEY'D DRIVEN MORE than a few miles, Sam had forced Holly to hand over her phone. He tossed it out the window into the snow, smiling over at her as he did so.

"We can't have you using that, now can we?"

Now they were at a rest stop, hundreds of miles away from Matt, and Holly desperately looked for a way to contact him. But there were no payphones, and she didn't have any money anyway. While Sam was in the bathroom, she considered running, but where could she go in all of this snow? Besides, Sam would catch her before she'd run a mile.

She considered, her mind whirling. What was Sam even planning? Would he kill her? She didn't know at this point, but she was well aware that Sam was unpredictable. As a last ditch effort, Holly ripped off a part of the coat—Matt's coat—and tied it to the light pole next to the only entrance to the rest stop. She had no idea if Matt would even come this way, but it was better than nothing.

She was sitting in the car by the time Sam returned. He got inside the car and they drove away, neither of them saying anything. Holly was so tired that she couldn't even feel fear anymore. Her cheek still hurt, though, from where Sam had slapped her, and it served as a reminder that no matter their history, she wasn't safe with this man.

They drove into the night. As dawn approached, they finally stopped at a little motel off the highway. Sam sent Holly to get food from the local diner next door, telling her if she tried anything, he'd kill her. Trembling and exhausted, she ordered food for them both. She almost told the waitress about her situation, but they were in the middle of nowhere. It would take who knew how long for the police to arrive, and if Sam saw them, he might snap and kill them both.

She returned to the motel room, an old, sparse room that smelled of cigarette smoke and sweat. She handed Sam his bacon and eggs, which he complained about and refused to eat after he discovered that the eggs were runny. Holly, for her part, could only drink coffee and nibble on a bagel.

Please find me, Matt, she kept praying. *Please find me. And don't die trying to get here.*

What if Matt didn't get up for hours, though? They'd be long gone by then, and it would be difficult to track them once they arrived in a big city like Kansas City. Holly bit the inside of her cheek to keep herself from sobbing outright.

Sam fell asleep, snoring, and Holly stared at the wall. The car keys were in his back pocket. If she tried to get them from his pocket, he could wake up and then there'd be trouble. But when he flipped over to his side, exposing said pocket, Holly decided she'd have to try. Moving toward him on the bed, she very slowly delved into his pocket, pulling out the keys and making sure they didn't jangle. Sam snorted in his sleep but didn't awaken.

Holly breathed a sigh of relief. She held the keys in her fist, but winced when the springs of the bed screeched. Sam continued sleeping, and she walked to the door with light steps. If she could just get this deadbolt off, and unlock the door, and open it…

"Going somewhere?" Sam slapped a hand against the door, boxing her in.

She didn't think. She reacted. Slamming her elbow into his stomach, he fell to the ground behind her. She wrenched open the door and ran for it, hearing him scream after her. She hadn't even put on her shoes, but it didn't matter. She had to get away. Making it to the car, she unlocked it, but as she was about to open the door, she was knocked to the ground. Sam was on top of her, and he backhanded her across the face so hard that she saw stars.

"You stupid bitch! Did you really think you'd get away from me?" He pulled her hair and took the keys from her hand.

Holly fought like a cat, clawing at him, refusing to let him take her back to that room. She screamed, but no one came out to help her.

She got in a slap, but Sam was stronger than her by fifty pounds. He flipped her over, smashing her face into the concrete, and he laughed.

"You're mine," he breathed, panting. "You're mine to do with whatever I want."

Holly couldn't breathe; she couldn't think. She just had to escape. She was about to buck him off, but before she could move, his weight was gone. Her mind couldn't comprehend what had had happened, but when she sat up, she saw that Sam was now on the ground with another man over him.

Matt. It was Matt.

Holly stood up, clutching at the car behind her. Matt kicked Sam in the ribs before forcing his arms behind his back. Pulling out cuffs, Matt said in a rough voice, "You're under arrest for assault and kidnapping and violating your restraining order. I'd recommend you not say anything else, Mr. Gantry."

Sam still tried to fight back, but he was no match for Matt. Matt called for backup, and another police officer took Sam into custody, escorting him to a nearby police car.

Holly kept blinking, she was so astonished. He'd found her. He'd saved her.

She ran to him and threw herself into his arms, and he hugged her so tightly she could barely breathe. She didn't care, though. He kept saying her name, his hands running down her body to make sure she was all right.

"Holly, God, Holly," he said into her hair. "Are you okay? If that bastard hurt you..."

She pulled away, and when he saw the growing bruise on her face, he growled. He cupped her cheek. "I'll kill him," he intoned.

She just hugged him tighter. "You found me. I didn't know if you would find me."

"Of course I would find you. I'd go to the ends of the earth for you." He tipped her head back to look into her eyes. "I love you, Holly. I know it's too early to say something like that, but I don't care. I only care about you."

She smiled, tears shining in her eyes. "I love you, Matt. Thank you for saving me."

He held her close, and he hugged her hard. "Why did you go with him? Why didn't you tell me? God, Holly, when we found your phone in the snow and then when you left a part of my coat at that rest stop…"

So he had found her clue. She smiled, but then she started sobbing. "I had to go with him, otherwise he was going to kill you. I couldn't take that chance."

Matt swore underneath his breath. "Don't ever do that again. Ever. I'm here to protect you. I don't care what happens to me. I'm only here to keep you safe, okay?"

And looking up into his eyes, she believed him with all of her heart.

EPILOGUE

One year later...

Christmastime meant two things to Holly Haldon: decorating the tree, and celebrating the day she and Matt became an official couple.

It had been an interesting year, given the trial (Sam was now in jail for at least twenty years), and then the engagement, and then their marriage three months ago. Matt hadn't wasted anytime in making Holly his wife, although she'd balked a little at the speed at which things had progressed. Shouldn't they date a while, she'd argued? But Matt, in his calm, Matt kind of way, had asked her why they should wait.

Since she couldn't give an answer, she eventually decided her boyfriend was right.

Now she gazed at the Christmas tree, smiling as she sipped her cup of eggnog. Who would've thought they'd both end up here after she'd gotten stuck in the snow one year ago?

"How are you feeling?" Matt sat down next to her, his arm around her shoulder. He leaned down to touch her abdomen, which had only just started to show the baby growing inside. "Feeling good today?"

She smiled. "I'm good. I only puked once this morning, and now I could eat the entire kitchen. Such is pregnancy, I've heard."

He rubbed her stomach, his face one of both awe and love. "I hate that you're feeling sick, but hopefully it won't last forever."

She covered his hand with hers. "For you and this baby, I'll put up with anything."

"Even my terrible singing?"

She grinned. "Even that." She kissed him, the kiss quickly turning into something more. Holly's body heated.

She'd assumed that pregnancy would make her libido pack up and go on hiatus. Apparently, though, she found her husband way too irresistible no matter how big her belly was. And lucky for her, he thought the same thing about her.

"I'm horny," said Holly, slightly annoyed. "Why am I still so horny all the time?"

Matt choked back a laugh. "That sounds like a terrible burden. I can do something about it, though."

She mock-sighed. "I mean, if you must."

His grin made her grin, and soon she was sitting on his lap, her belly making things a bit awkward. Matt gripped her hair and tilted her head to the side so he could kiss her neck. His other hand had already moved under her shirt to rub her back. She waited for him to play with her breasts—ultra-sensitive now—but he just kept kissing her and running his fingers down her spine.

"You're killing me," she muttered.

"Patience is a virtue."

She rolled her eyes, but then both of Matt's hands were cupping her breasts. His thumbs brushed across her nipples, making Holly shiver with want. She didn't know how he managed to get her going so quickly, but she couldn't complain.

Matt kissed her, playing with her breasts until Holly began to squirm. He soothed her and whispered that he'd take care of her. He'd always take care of her.

Holly tried to unzip Matt's jeans, but her belly made it too awkward. Matt laughed. "Need some help?"

She growled. "No, I think I got it—" Except she couldn't unbutton his jeans without getting off of his lap. Considering that getting herself off of the couch and out of bed was basically an Olympic sport at this point, she was determined to get him out of his jeans without her moving.

"Baby, let me do it." He brushed her hands away and soon his cock was freed. Holly was glad that she was only wearing a dress—yes, even in winter. The pregnancy gave her heat flashes, one of the sexier side effects.

After some maneuvering and laughter, Holly sunk down onto Matt, the two of them groaning together. Holly gripped his shoulders as she began to grind on him. She couldn't really ride him, but they'd quickly discovered that a slow grind felt just as good to them both.

Matt gripped her ass at the same time that he lifted his hips to push against her. Holly let out a moan. She was already close—painfully close.

Matt sucked on the side of her neck as her release slammed into her. She bit her lip, but it didn't stop her from swearing as she groaned. Matt grunted and came moments later. He pressed his mouth to hers and kissed her hard as they both tried to catch their breath.

After they cleaned up and got dressed again, Holly sat in the circle of Matt's arms, humming as she finished knitting some booties. She'd never knitted in her life until she'd found out she was pregnant. At the moment, she was terrible at it, and the booties looked more like vague circles that wouldn't hold much of anything. But she didn't care. She was in love, and with the man who loved her, and they would have a baby come summer.

Everything was perfect.

"Look, Holly." Matt pointed, and she glanced out the window to see snowflakes falling. "I guess we'll have a white Christmas."

She got up to go to the window, the dogs following. Matt stood behind her as they gazed out onto the snowy landscape.

"I love you." He kissed the top of her head.

Holly smiled, leaning against him. His arms held her close. "I love you, too. Thank you for finding me."

He lifted her face so they could look into each other's eyes. "Didn't you know, sweetheart? You were the one who found me."

ABOUT THE AUTHOR

A coffee addict and cat lover, Iris Morland writes sexy and funny contemporary romances. If she's not reading or writing, she enjoys binging on Netflix shows and cooking something delicious.

irismorland.com